MW01634553

SHAKESPEARE

OTHELLO

REVIEW QUESTIONS AND ANSWERS

COLES EDITORIAL BOARD

Publisher's Note

Otabind (Ota-bind). This book has been bound using the patented Otabind process. You can open this book at any page, gently run your finger down the spine, and the pages will lie flat.

ABOUT COLES NOTES

COLES NOTES have been an indispensible aid to students on five continents since 1948.

COLES NOTES are available for a wide range of individual literary works. Clear, concise explanations and insights are provided along with interesting interpretations and evaluations.

Proper use of COLES NOTES will allow the student to pay greater attention to lectures and spend less time taking notes. This will result in a broader understanding of the work being studied and will free the student for increased participation in discussions.

COLES NOTES are an invaluable aid for review and exam preparation as well as an invitation to explore different interpretive paths.

COLES NOTES are written by experts in their fields. It should be noted that any literary judgement expressed herein is just that – the judgement of one school of thought. Interpretations that diverge from, or totally disagree with any criticism may be equally valid.

COLES NOTES are designed to supplement the text and are not intended as a substitute for reading the text itself. Use of the NOTES will serve not only to clarify the work being studied, but should enhance the readers enjoyment of the topic.

ISBN 0-7740-3782-2

© COPYRIGHT 1999 AND PUBLISHED BY
COLES PUBLISHING COMPANY
TORONTO—CANADA
PRINTED IN CANADA

Manufactured by Webcom Limited
Cover finish: Webcom's Exclusive **DURACOAT**

CONTENTS

Page No.

Part A:
The Play in Brief
INTRODUCTION 1
CHARACTERS IN THE PLAY 1

Part B:
Questions and Answers by Act and Scene 36

Part C:
General Review Questions and Answers 60

Part A: The Play in Brief

Introduction

As enjoyable and important as Shakespeare's plays are, they can be difficult to read. Since Shakespeare wrote his plays to appeal to Elizabethan audiences, much of the text is dated and means little to the average reader of today.

We are, therefore, presenting the substance of the play in readable form by eliminating, as much as possible, the outdated passages and by paraphrasing the more complicated ones. This will give you a better understanding and appreciation of the play, and will make the questions and answers more meaningful.

CHARACTERS IN THE PLAY

Othello: A noble Moor serving the Venetian state.
Brabantio: A Venetian senator.
Cassio: Othello's lieutenant.
Iago: A villain.
Roderigo: A Venetian gentleman.
Duke of Venice
Montano: Governor of Cyprus.
Gratiano: Brabantio's brother.
Lodovico: Brabantio's kinsman.
Clown
Desdemona: Brabantio's daughter; Othello's wife.
Emilia: Iago's wife.
Bianca: Cassio's mistress.
Senators, Sailors, Messenger, Herald, Officers, Gentlemen, Musicians and Attendants.

[Setting: Venice and Cyprus.]

ACT I

On a dimly lit street in Venice, Roderigo and Iago are talking. Roderigo is upset because, although he bribed Iago to help him in his courtship of Desdemona, Senator Brabantio's beautiful daughter, the woman has just eloped with Othello, a Moor and the general of the Venetian army.

In order to maintain Roderigo's confidence, as well as control of the young man's money, Iago tells him that he also has reasons for resenting Othello. Iago explains how Othello denied him a promotion and appointed Cassio as his lieutenant instead:

> Three great ones of the city,
> In personal suit to make me his lieutenant,
> Off-capp'd to him: and, by the faith of man,
> I know my price, I am worth no worse a place:
> But he, as loving his own pride and purposes,
> Evades them, with a bombast circumstance
> Horribly stuff'd with epithets of war;
> And, in conclusion,
> Nonsuits my mediators; for, 'Certes,' says he,
> 'I have already chose my officer.'
> And what was he?
> Forsooth, a great arithmetician,
> One Michael Cassio, a Florentine,
> A fellow almost damn'd in a fair wife;
> That never set a squadron in the field,
> Nor the division of a battle knows
> More than a spinster; unless the bookish theoric,
> Wherein the toged consuls can propose
> As masterly as he: mere prattle without practice
> Is all his soldiership. But he, sir, had the election:
> And I, of whom his eyes had seen the proof
> At Rhodes, at Cyprus, and on other grounds
> Christian and heathen, must be be-lee'd and calm'd
> By debitor and creditor: this counter-caster,
> He, in good time, must his lieutenant be,
> And I — God bless the mark! — his Moorship's ancient.
> **Roderigo:** By heaven, I rather would have been his hangman.

Iago: Why, there's no remedy; 'tis the curse of
service,
Preferment goes by letter and affection,
And not by old gradation, where each second
Stood heir to the first. Now, sir, be judge yourself
Whether I in any just term am affined
To love the Moor.

Iago, having quieted Roderigo's complaints, suggests that the young man awaken Desdemona's father and tell him about his daughter's elopement. Roderigo and Iago awaken Brabantio with their cries. Brabantio, half asleep, appears at the window and accuses Roderigo of being drunk and disturbing the peace. Roderigo finally manages to tell Brabantio the news about his daughter, with Iago adding his crude comments: "Even now, now, very now, an old black ram/Is tupping your white ewe."

Brabantio is quite distressed:

O heaven! How got she out? O treason of the blood!
Fathers, from hence trust not your daughters' minds
By what you see them act. Is there not charms
By which the property of youth and maidhood
May be abused?

Although Brabantio had earlier forbidden Roderigo to enter his house, the senator now enlists Roderigo's help to find the eloped couple.

The next scene opens with Iago hypocritically claiming his loyalty to Othello and accusing Roderigo of speaking against the Moor:

Though in the trade of war I have slain men,
Yet do I hold it very stuff o' the conscience
To do no contrived murder: I lack iniquity
Sometimes to do me service: nine or ten times
I had thought to have yerk'd him here under the ribs
Othello: 'Tis better as it is.
Iago: Nay, but he prated
And spoke such scurvy and provoking terms
Against your honour,

That, with the little godliness I have,
I did full hard forbear him.

He then asks Othello whether he is really married and to warn him about Brabantio, a man of great power in Venice. Othello replies that, in his own land, he is the equal in birth of any Venetian.

Then, Othello sees the torches of another group, which turns out to be his lieutenant, Cassio, with officers, seeking him because the Duke desires his advice concerning reports of a Turkish invasion of Cyprus. They are interrupted by the appearance of Brabantio and his friends. As each party draws its swords, Othello speaks with authority:

Keep up your bright swords, for the dew will rust
them.
Good signior, you shall more command with years
Than with your weapons.

Brabantio speaks angrily to Othello:

O thou foul thief, where hast thou stow'd my
daughter?
Damn'd as thou art, thou hast enchanted her;
For I'll refer me to all things of sense,
If she in chains of magic were not bound,
Whether a maid so tender, fair and happy,
So opposite to marriage that she shunn'd
The wealthy curled darlings of our nation,
Would ever have, to incur a general mock,
Run from her guardage to the sooty bosom
Of such a thing as thou, to fear, not to delight.
Judge me the world, if 'tis not gross in sense
That thou hast practised on her with foul charms,
Abused her delicate youth with drugs or minerals
That weaken motion: I'll have 't disputed on;
'Tis probable, and palpable to thinking.
I therefore apprehend and do attach thee
For an abuser of the world, a practiser
Of arts inhibited and out of warrant.
Lay hold upon him: if he do resist,

Subdue him at his peril.

Hearing that Othello is on his way to see the Duke, Brabantio decides to accompany him so that he can present his case against the Moor immediately.

The next scene takes place in the council chamber, where the Duke and senators are receiving constant reports from Cyprus about the Turkish fleet that is heading there. When Othello and Brabantio come in, Brabantio immediately breaks into speech about his daughter, who, he says, was taken from him through evil spells:

> She is abused, stol'n from me and corrupted
> By spells and medicines bought of mountebanks;
> For nature so preposterously to err,
> Being not deficient, blind, or lame of sense,
> Sans witchcraft could not.

The Duke's reply is sympathetic:

> Whoe'er he be that in this foul proceeding
> Hath thus beguiled your daughter of herself
> And you of her, the bloody book of law
> You shall yourself read in the bitter letter
> After your own sense, yea, though our proper son
> Stood in your action.

After learning that Othello is the offender, the Duke turns to hear the Moor's defence. Othello explains his actions:

> Most potent, grave, and reverend signiors,
> My very noble and approved good masters,
> That I have ta'en away this old man's daughter,
> It is most true; true, I have married her:
> The very head and front of my offending
> Hath this extent, no more. Rude am I in my speech,
> And little blest with the soft phrase of peace;
> For since these arms of mine had seven years' pith,
> Till now some nine moons wasted, they have used
> Their dearest action in the tented field;
> And little of this great world can I speak,

More than pertains to feats of broil and battle;
And therefore little shall I grace my cause
In speaking for myself. Yet, by your gracious
patience,
I will a round unvarnish'd tale deliver
Of my whole course of love; what drugs, what charms,
What conjuration and what mighty magic
For such proceeding I am charged withal
I won his daughter.

Brabantio continues to insist that Othello used "practices of
cunning hell" to charm his daughter, but the Duke notes that "To
vouch this, is no proof." Othello suggests that Desdemona be
brought in and questioned in person.
While they wait for Desdemona, Othello explains "How I did
thrive in this fair lady's blood/And she in mine:"

Her father loved me, oft invited me,
Still question'd me the story of my life
From year to year, the battles, sieges, fortunes,
That I have pass'd.
I ran it through, even from my boyish days
To the very moment that he bade me tell it:
Wherein I spake of most disastrous chances,
Of moving accidents by flood and field,
Of hair-breadth 'scapes i' the imminent deadly breach,
Of being taken by the insolent foe,
And sold to slavery, of my redemption thence,
And portance in my travels' history:
Wherein of antres vast and deserts idle,
Rough quarries, rocks, and hills whose heads touch
heaven,
It was my hint to speak, such was the process;
And of the Cannibals that each other eat,
The Anthropophagi, and men whose heads
Do grow beneath their shoulders. This to hear
Would Desdemona seriously incline.
But still the house-affairs would draw her thence;
Which ever as she could with haste dispatch,
She'ld come again, and with a greedy ear
Devour up my discourse, which I observing,

Took once a pliant hour, and found good means
To draw from her a prayer of earnest heart
That I would all my pilgrimage dilate,
Whereof by parcels she had something heard,
But not intentively. I did consent,
And often did beguile her of her tears
When I did speak of some distressful stroke
That my youth suffer'd. My story being done,
She gave me for my pains a world of sighs.
She swore, in faith, 'twas strange, 'twas passing
strange;
'Twas pitiful, 'twas wondrous pitiful.
She wish'd she had not heard it, yet she wish'd
That heaven had made her such a man. She thank'd
me,
And bade me, if I had a friend that loved her,
I should but teach him how to tell my story,
And that would woo her. Upon this hint I spake:
She loved me for the dangers I had pass'd,
And I loved her that she did pity them.
This only is the witchcraft I have used.

Desdemona enters, and Brabantio says:

I pray you, hear her speak:
If she confess that she was half the wooer,
Destruction on my head, if my bad blame
Light on the man! Come hither, gentle mistress:
Do you perceive in all this noble company
Where most you owe obedience?

Desdemona explains the "divided duty" she owes to
Brabantio and to Othello. She tells her father:

To you I am bound for life and education;
My life and education both do learn me
How to respect you; you are the lord of duty,
I am hitherto your daughter: but here's my husband,
And so much duty as my mother show'd
To you, preferring you before her father,
So much I challenge that I may profess

Due to the Moor my lord.

Satisfied that his daughter was not bewitched into marrying
Othello, Brabantio tells his new son-in-law:

I here do give thee that with all my heart,
Which, but thou hast already, with all my heart
I would keep from thee.

The Duke contributes a few words of advice, directed chiefly
at Brabantio:

When remedies are past, the griefs are ended
By seeing the worst, which late on hopes depended.
To mourn a mischief that is past and gone
Is the next way to draw new mischief on.
What cannot be preserved when fortune takes,
Patience her injury a mockery makes.
The robb'd that smiles steals something from the thief;
He robs himself that spends a bootless grief.

Brabantio urges the Duke to proceed with public business.
The Duke then tells Othello about the Turkish threat to Cyprus and
asks Othello to take charge of the defence of that island. Othello
agrees, asking only that Desdemona be properly cared for during
his absence. Desdemona wishes to accompany her husband, rather
than return to her father's home, and Othello supports her plea. The
Duke and the senators grant this request and order Othello to leave
for Cyprus that night. They also decide that a trustworthy officer
will be in charge of bringing Othello further orders and conducting
Desdemona to Cyprus later. Othello suggests Iago for the job:

A man he is of honesty and trust.
To his conveyance I assign my wife.

As the Duke and the senators are leaving, Brabantio offers
Othello some parting advice:

Look to her, Moor, if thou hast eyes to see:
She has deceived her father, and may thee.

''My life upon her faith,'' replies Othello, who then asks Iago to see that Desdemona is attended by Emilia, Iago's wife. Othello and Desdemona leave.

Iago is left alone with Roderigo, who is in despair about losing Desdemona. Iago is disgusted, having little patience for a lover's complaints. When Roderigo sadly admits that it is not his ''virtue'' to be able to overcome his feelings of love, Iago scornfully replies:

> Virtue! a fig! 'tis in ourselves that we are thus or thus. Our bodies are gardens; to the which our wills are gardeners: that if we will plant nettles or sow lettuce, set hyssop and weed up thyme, supply it with one gender of herbs or distract it with many, either to have it sterile with idleness or manured with industry, why, the power and corrigible authority of this lies in our wills. If the balance of our lives had not one scale of reason to poise another of sensuality, the blood and baseness of our natures would conduct us to most preposterous conclusions: but we have reason to cool our raging motions, our carnal stings, our unbitted lusts; whereof I take this, that you call love, to be a sect or scion.

Iago then boosts Roderigo's hopes:

> It is merely a lust of the blood and a permission of the will. Come, be a man: drown thyself! drown cats and blind puppies. I have professed me thy friend, and I confess me knit to thy deserving with cables of perdurable toughness: I could never better stead thee than now. Put money in thy purse; follow thou the wars; defeat thy favour with an usurped beard; I say, put money in thy purse. It cannot be that Desdemona should long continue her love to the Moor—put money in thy purse—nor he his to her: it was a violent commencement, and thou shalt see an answerable sequestration; put but money in thy purse. These Moors are changeable in their wills:—fill thy purse with money. The food that to him now is as luscious as locusts, shall be to him shortly as bitter as coloquintida. She must change for youth: when she is sated with his body, she will find the error of her choice: she must have change, she must: therefore put money in thy purse. If

thou wilt needs damn thyself, do it a more delicate way
than drowning. Make all the money thou canst: if sanc-
timony and a frail vow betwixt an erring barbarian and a
supersubtle Venetian be not too hard for my wits and all
the tribe of hell, thou shalt enjoy her; therefore make
money. A pox of drowning thyself! it is clean out of the
way: seek thou rather to be hanged in compassing thy joy
than to be drowned and go without her.

Roderigo goes to raise what money he can, leaving Iago to his
thoughts:

Thus do I ever make my fool my purse;
For I mine own gain'd knowledge should profane,
If I would time expend with such a snipe
But for my sport and profit. I hate the Moor;
And it is thought abroad that 'twixt my sheets
He has done my office: I know not if 't be true;
But I for mere suspicion in that kind
Will do as if for surety. He holds me well;
The better shall my purpose work on him.
Cassio's a proper man: let me see now;
To get his place, and to plume up my will
In double knavery — How, how? — Let's see:
After some time, to abuse Othello's ear
That he is too familiar with his wife.
He hath a person and a smooth dispose
To be suspected; framed to make women false.
The Moor is of a free and open nature,
That thinks men honest that but seem to be so;
And will as tenderly be led by the nose
As asses are.
I have 't. It is engender'd. Hell and night
Must bring this monstrous birth to the world's light.

ACT II

It is some days later on the island of Cyprus. There has been a terrible storm at sea that has destroyed the Turkish fleet, so that the prospect of war has vanished. But everyone is anxious to learn how Othello's fleet has managed. One ship, carrying Cassio, arrives, and he tells Montano, the officer in charge in Cyprus, that he has lost track of Othello at sea. A second ship, carrying Iago and Desdemona, lands. Cassio has told Montano about her marriage. She is welcomed warmly, just as the cannons are heard saluting a third ship. Meanwhile, Iago puts his own interpretation upon Cassio's courteous welcome to Desdemona:

He takes her by the palm: ay, well said, whisper: with as little a web as this will I ensnare as great a fly as Cassio. Ay, smile upon her, do; I will gyve thee in thine own courtship. You say true; 'tis so, indeed: if such tricks as these strip you out of your lieutenantry, it had been better you had not kissed your three fingers so oft, which now again you are most apt to play the sir in. Very good; well kissed! an excellent courtesy! 'tis so, indeed. Yet again your fingers to your lips? Would they were clyster-pipes for your sake! *[Trumpet within.]* The Moor! I know his trumpet.

Othello appears. He is greatly surprised to see Desdemona there before him, and they greet each other affectionately. Seeing them kiss, Iago says to himself:

O, you are well tuned now!
But I'll set down the pegs that make this music,
As honest as I am.

As they go to the castle, Iago is ordered to supervise the unloading of Othello's baggage, but he remains behind for a moment to talk to Roderigo about Cassio:

Do thou meet me presently at the harbour. Come hither.
If thou be'st valiant—as, they say, base men being in love
have then a nobility in their natures more than is native to

them — list me. The lieutenant to-night watches on the court of guard. First, I must tell thee this: Desdemona is directly in love with him.

Roderigo: With him! why, 'tis not possible.

Iago: Lay thy finger thus, and let thy soul be instructed. Mark me with what violence she first loved the Moor, but for bragging and telling her fantastical lies: and will she love him still for prating? let not thy discreet heart think it. Her eye must be fed; and what delight shall she have to look on the devil? When the blood is made dull with the act of sport, there should be, again to inflame it and to give satiety a fresh appetite, loveliness in favour, sympathy in years, manners and beauties; all which the Moor is defective in. Now, for want of these required conveniences, her delicate tenderness will find itself abused, begin to heave the gorge, disrelish and abhor the Moor; very nature will instruct her in it and compel her to some second choice. Now, sir, this granted — as it is a most pregnant and unforced position — who stands so eminently in the degree of this fortune as Cassio does? A knave very voluble; no further conscionable than in putting on the mere form of civil and humane seeming, for the better compassing of his salt and most hidden loose affection? Why, none; why, none: a slipper and subtle knave; a finder out of occasions; that has an eye can stamp and counterfeit advantages, though true advantage never present itself: a devilish knave! Besides, the knave is handsome, young, and hath all those requisites in him that folly and green minds look after: a pestilent complete knave; and the woman hath found him already.

Roderigo is easily fooled by Iago into believing that Cassio and Desdemona are lovers. Roderigo is thus persuaded to help in getting rid of his new rival. Iago's scheme is to have Roderigo annoy Cassio ''by speaking too loud, or tainting his discipline.'' The hot-tempered Cassio probably will attack Roderigo, and Iago will use this quarrel to have the Cyprians mutiny against Cassio and demand his dismissal.

When Roderigo has gone, Iago reveals the full extent of his plans:

That Cassio loves her, I do well believe it;
That she loves him, 'tis apt and of great credit:
The Moor, howbeit that I endure him not,
Is of a constant, loving, noble nature;
And I dare think he'll prove to Desdemona
A most dear husband. Now, I do love her too,
Not out of absolute lust, though peradventure
I stand accountant for as great a sin,
But partly led to diet my revenge,
For that I do suspect the lusty Moor
Hath leap'd into my seat: the thought whereof
Doth like a poisonous mineral gnaw my inwards;
And nothing can or shall content my soul
Till I am even'd with him, wife for wife;
Or failing so, yet that I put the Moor
At least into a jealousy so strong
That judgement cannot cure. Which thing to do,
If this poor trash of Venice, whom I trash
For his quick hunting, stand the putting on,
I'll have our Michael Cassio on the hip,
Abuse him to the Moor in the rank garb;
For I fear Cassio with my night-cap too;
Make the Moor thank me, love me and reward me,
For making him egregiously an ass
And practising upon his peace and quiet
Even to madness. 'Tis here, but yet confused:
Knavery's plain face is never seen till used.

That night is declared a holiday in celebration of the destruction of the Turkish fleet and the marriage of Othello and Desdemona. During the festivities, Othello cautions Cassio to keep
on eye on the guards and see that the merriment does not interfere
with the carrying out of their duties. Cassio reminds Othello that
Iago is in charge. Othello describes Iago as an ''honest man'' as he
leaves with Desdemona.

Iago enters soon after and invites Cassio to join him and a few
other men in drinking to Othello's health. Cassio refuses at first,
but he eventually decides to join in after all. When Cassio leaves,
Iago reveals his plans:

If I can fasten but one cup upon him,

With that which he hath drunk to-night already,
He'll be as full of quarrel and offence
As my young mistress' dog. Now my sick fool
Roderigo,
Whom love hath turn'd almost the wrong side out,
To Desdemona hath to-night caroused
Potations pottle-deep; and he's to watch:
Three lads of Cyprus, noble swelling spirits,
That hold their honours in a wary distance,
The very elements of this warlike isle,
Have I to-night fluster'd with flowing cups,
And they watch too. Now, 'mongst this flock of
drunkards,
Am I to put our Cassio in some action
That may offend the isle. But here they come:
If consequence do but approve my dream,
My boat sails freely, both with wind and stream.

When Cassio returns, Montano and three young Cypriot men
are with him. Iago tempts them to further drinking. When Cassio
finally goes out to stand guard, Iago turns to Montano:

You see this fellow that is gone before;
He is a soldier fit to stand by Caesar
And give direction: and do but see his vice;
'Tis to his virtue a just equinox,
The one as long as the other: 'tis pity of him.
I fear the trust Othello puts him in
On some odd time of his infirmity
Will shake this island.

Iago's conversation with Montano is interrupted when Cassio
rushes in pursuing Roderigo. Montano tries to stop Cassio and is
wounded. This struggle gives Iago the opportunity to send
Roderigo to sound the alarm bell. Its noise arouses Othello, who
comes to quiet the disturbance. After questioning each man unsuccessfully, he angrily declares:

Now, by heaven,
My blood begins my safer guides to rule,
And passion, having my best judgement collied,

Assays to lead the way: if I once stir,
Or do but lift this arm, the best of you
Shall sink in my rebuke. Give me to know
How this foul rout began, who set it on,
And he that is approved in this offence,
Though he had twinn'd with me, both at a birth,
Shall lose me. What! in a town of war,
Yet wild, the people's hearts brimful of fear,
To manage private and domestic quarrel,
In night, and on the court and guard of safety!
'Tis monstrous. Iago, who began 't?

Protesting that he would rather have his tongue cut out than use it to harm Cassio, Iago cleverly describes what happened to show Cassio in the worst possible light. Othello, completely deceived, tells Iago, ''Thy honesty and love doth mince this matter,/ Making it light to Cassio.''

Desdemona enters and asks what the disturbance is all about. Othello leads her away, along with the wounded Montano, leaving Iago to restore peace.

Alone with Cassio, Iago pretends to be concerned about the lieutenant's wounds. But what really hurts Cassio is the loss of his reputation, a matter that Iago treats lightly:

Cassio: Reputation, reputation, reputation! O, I have lost my reputation! I have lost the immortal part of myself, and what remains is bestial. My reputation, Iago, my reputation!

Iago: As I am an honest man, I thought you had received some bodily wound; there is more sense in that than in reputation. Reputation is an idle and most false imposition; oft got without merit and lost without deserving: you have lost no reputation at all, unless you repute yourself such a loser. What, man! there are ways to recover the general again: you are but now cast in his mood, a punishment more in policy than in malice; even so as one would beat his offenceless dog to affright an imperious lion: sue to him again, and he's yours.

Cassio cannot recall any of his drunken actions clearly, but he feels deeply ashamed nevertheless. When Cassio doubts that

Othello will give him back his position, Iago slyly suggests that he appeal to Desdemona to use her influence in trying to persuade Othello to be lenient. "You advise me well," Cassio tells Iago. Cassio plans to speak to Desdemona in the morning.

Left alone, Iago congratulates himself for his successful plotting:

> And what's he then that says I play the villain?
> When this advice is free I give and honest,
> Probal to thinking, and indeed the course
> To win the Moor again? For 'tis most easy
> The inclining Desdemona to subdue
> In any honest suit. She's framed as fruitful
> As the free elements. And then for her
> To win the Moor, were 't to renounce his baptism,
> All seals and symbols of redeemed sin,
> His soul is so enfetter'd to her love,
> That she may makc, unmake, do what she list,
> Even as her appetite shall play the god
> With his weak function. How am I then a villain
> To counsel Cassio to this parallel course,
> Directly to his good? Divinity of hell!
> When devils will the blackest sins put on,
> They do suggest at first with heavenly shows,
> As I do now: for whiles this honest fool
> Plies Desdemona to repair his fortunes,
> And she for him pleads strongly to the Moor,
> I'll pour this pestilence into his ear,
> That she repeals him for her body's lust;
> And by how much she strives to do him good,
> She shall undo her credit with the Moor.
> So will I turn her virtue into pitch;
> And out of her own goodness make the net
> That shall enmesh them all.

Roderigo enters, complaining that nothing is going well for him. "With no money at all and a little more wit," he plans to return to Venice. Iago convinces Roderigo to be patient. When Roderigo leaves, Iago continues his evil scheming:

> Two things are to be done:

My wife must move for Cassio to her mistress;
I'll set her on;
Myself the while to draw the Moor apart,
And bring him jump when he may Cassio find
Soliciting his wife: ay, that's the way;
Dull not device by coldness and delay.

ACT III

There is now a brief period of relief from the mounting tragedy as Cassio arranges for some musicians to play before the castle the next morning. Othello has sent a clown to dismiss the musicians, and Cassio uses this clown as his messenger to ask Emilia, Iago's wife, to come outside and speak to him.

Iago enters and promises to send Emilia to Cassio and to distract Othello while they talk.

Emilia enters soon after Iago leaves. Cassio begs her, "Give me advantage of some brief discourse/With Desdemona alone." Emilia agrees to assist him.

While Othello is away inspecting his fortifications, Cassio and Desdemona meet. She assures him that she will help his cause in any way she can. When Emilia announces Othello's approach, Cassio, ashamed of his conduct the night before, rushes away. Iago sees this and exclaims:

> Ha! I like not that.
> **Othello:** What dost thou say?
> **Iago:** Nothing, my lord: or if — I know not what.
> **Othello:** Was not that Cassio parted from my wife?
> **Iago:** Cassio, my lord! No, sure, I cannot think it,
> That he would steal away so guilty-like,
> Seeing you coming.
> **Othello:** I do believe 'twas he.

Desdemona immediately tells Othello that she has been speaking to Cassio and she goes on to plead Cassio's cause. Although Othello shows no interest in Cassio right now, Desdemona is persistent in attempting to arrange a time when Othello can meet with the young man. Othello finally agrees to "let him come when he will," adding, "I will deny thee nothing." He then asks her to leave him alone for a while.

When Desdemona and Emilia have gone, Iago cleverly begins to create a sense of suspicion and uneasiness in Othello's mind. Iago makes no direct accusations against Desdemona and Cassio, but, by giving Othello the impression that he knows more than he is saying, he leads the Moor to exclaim:

By heaven, he echoes me,
As if there were some monster in his thought
Too hideous to be shown.

Iago continues to play on Othello's suspicions, finally warning him to beware of jealousy, exactly the emotion the villain wishes to excite in Othello:

O, beware, my lord, of jealousy;
It is the green-eyed monster, which doth mock
The meat it feeds on: that cuckold lives in bliss
Who, certain of his fate, loves not his wronger;
But, O, what damned minutes tells he o'er
Who dotes, yet doubts, suspects, yet strongly loves!
Othello: O misery!
Iago: Poor and content is rich, and rich enough;
But riches fineless is as poor as winter
To him that ever fears he shall be poor:
Good heaven, the souls of all my tribe defend
From jealousy!

But Othello assures Iago:

I'll see before I doubt; when I doubt, prove;
And on the proof, there is no more but this,
Away at once with love or jealousy!
Iago: I am glad of it; for now I shall have reason
To show the love and duty that I bear you
With franker spirit: therefore, as I am bound,
Receive it from me. I speak not yet of proof.
Look to your wife: observe her well with Cassio;
Wear your eye thus, not jealous nor secure:
I would not have your free and noble nature
Out of self-bounty be abused; look to 't:
I know our country disposition well;
In Venice they do let heaven see the pranks
They dare not show their husbands; their best conscience
Is not to leave 't undone, but keep 't unknown.

Iago then reminds Othello that Desdemona has practised deception before:

She did deceive her father, marrying you;
And when she seem'd to shake and fear your looks,
She loved them most.

Iago goes on to suggest that, since Desdemona has shown a certain willfulness in choosing Othello, a Moor, as her husband instead of someone of her own color, she may show "unnatural" tendencies in other respects.

Thoroughly confused and upset, Othello cries out:

Why did I marry? This honest creature doubtless
Sees and knows more, much more, than he unfolds.

Othello, before dismissing Iago, asks him to continue to report to him any suspicious activities on Desdemona's part. Iago leaves and then returns in a moment to suggest that Othello refuse to see Cassio for awhile:

Though it be fit that Cassio have his place,
For sure he fills it up with great ability,
Yet, if you please to hold him off awhile,
You shall by that perceive him and his means:
Note if your lady strain his entertainment
With any strong or vehement importunity;
Much will be seen in that.

When Iago has left a second time, Othello remarks:

This fellow's of exceeding honesty,
And knows all qualities, with a learned spirit,
Of human dealings. If I do prove her haggard,
Though that her jesses were my dear heart-strings,
I'ld whistle her off and let her down the wind
To prey at fortune. Haply, for I am black
And have not those soft parts of conversation
That chamberers have, or for I am declined
Into the vale of years — yet that's not much —
She's gone; I am abused, and my relief

Must be to loathe her. O curse of marriage,
That we can call these delicate creatures ours,
And not their appetites! I had rather be a toad,
And live upon the vapour of a dungeon,
Than keep a corner in the thing I love
For others' uses. Yet, 'tis the plague of great ones;
Prerogatived are they less than the base;
'Tis destiny unshunnable, like death:
Even then this forked plague is fated to us
When we do quicken. Desdemona comes:
        [Re-enter Desdemona and Emilia.]
If she be false, O, then heaven mocks itself!
I'll not believe 't.

Desdemona has come to remind Othello that the guests he has invited to dinner have arrived. When he says he has a headache, she tries to bind his head with her handkerchief. It is too small, and, unnoticed, it drops on the ground. As she goes out with Othello, Emilia picks the handkerchief up, saying to herself:

I am glad I have found this napkin:
This was her first remembrance from the Moor:
My wayward husband hath a hundred times
Woo'd me to steal it; but she so loves the token,
For he conjured her she should ever keep it,
That she reserves it evermore about her
To kiss and talk to. I'll have the work ta'en out,
And give 't Iago: what he will do with it
Heaven knows, not I;
I nothing but to please his fantasy.

Iago appears and, snatching the handkerchief from her, sends her away with the command to keep the whole thing secret. He has plans for its use:

I will in Cassio's lodging lose this napkin,
And let him find it. Trifles light as air
Are to the jealous confirmations strong
As proofs of holy writ: this may do something.
The Moor already changes with my poison:
Dangerous conceits are in their natures poisons,

Which at the first are scarce found to distaste,
But with a little act upon the blood
Burn like the mines of sulphur. I did say so:
Look, where he comes!
Not poppy, nor mandragora,
Nor all the drowsy syrups of the world,
Shall ever medicine thee to that sweet sleep
Which thou owedst yesterday.

By now, Othello is convinced that Iago's accusations are true.
Othello enters, raving:

What sense had I of her stol'n hours of lust?
I saw 't not, thought it not, it harm'd not me:
I slept the next night well, was free and merry;
I found not Cassio's kisses on her lips:
He that is robb'd, not wanting what is stol'n,
Let him not know 't and he's not robb'd at all.
Iago: I am sorry to hear this.
Othello: I had been happy, if the general camp,
Pioneers and all, had tasted her sweet body,
So I had nothing known. O, now for ever
Farewell the tranquil mind! farewell content!
Farewell the plumed troop and the big wars
That make ambition virtue! O, farewell,
Farewell the neighing steed and the shrill trump,
The spirit-stirring drum, the ear-piercing fife,
The royal banner and all quality,
Pride, pomp and circumstance of glorious war!
And, O you mortal engines, whose rude throats
The immortal Jove's dread clamours counterfeit,
Farewell! Othello's occupation's gone!

But Othello asks Iago to provide him with definite proof of
Desdemona's unfaithfulness:

Villain, be sure thou prove my love a whore;
Be sure of it; give me the ocular proof;
Or, by the worth of man's eternal soul,
Thou hadst been better have been born a dog
Than answer my waked wrath!

Othello warns Iago that the proof must be absolute ''or woe upon thy life!'' Iago protests that such threats are no reward for his honesty. Pretending to be deeply offended, Iago says:

To be direct and honest is not safe.
I thank you for this profit, and from hence
I'll love no friend sith love breeds such offence.

Othello calms down enough to urge Iago not to leave, adding, ''thou shouldst be honest.'' Iago expresses false concern for Othello:

I see, sir, you are eaten up with passion:
I do repent me that I put it to you.

Iago now offers Othello the definite proof he is after. He tells Othello that he heard Cassio talking in his sleep about making love to Desdemona. Othello, deeply affected, exclaims, ''I'll tear her all to pieces.'' Then, Iago introduces his strongest piece of evidence: the handkerchief ''spotted with strawberries.'' Iago claims that he has often seen Cassio wiping his beard with this handkerchief.

Othello is now convinced. Although Iago advises him to be patient — ''Your mind perhaps may change'' — Othello swears he will have revenge. Iago solemnly promises to assist him in this cause:

Othello: Never, Iago. Like to the Pontic sea,
Whose icy current and compulsive course
Ne'er feels retiring ebb, but keeps due on
To the Propontic and the Hellespont;
Even so my bloody thoughts, with violent pace,
Shall ne'er look back, ne'er ebb to humble love,
Till that a capable and wide revenge
Swallow them up. Now, by yond marble heaven,
In the due reverence of a sacred vow   *[Kneels.]*
I here engage my words.
Iago: Do not rise yet.   *[Kneels.]*
Witness, you ever-burning lights above,
You elements that clip us round about,
Witness that here Iago doth give up

The execution of his wit, hands, heart,
To wrong'd Othello's service! Let him command,
And to obey shall be in me remorse,
What bloody business ever.   *[They rise.]*
Othello: I greet thy love,
Not with vain thanks, but with acceptance bounteous,
And will upon the instant put thee to 't:
Within these three days let me hear thee say
That Cassio's not alive.
Iago: My friend is dead; 'tis done at your request:
But let her live.
Othello: Damn her, lewd minx! O, damn her!
Come, go with me apart; I will withdraw,
To furnish me with some swift means of death
For the fair devil. Now art thou my lieutenant.
Iago: I am your own for ever.

Meanwhile, Desdemona is asking the clown to find Cassio. She is sure she has persuaded Othello to forgive the lieutenant. Desdemona turns to Emilia after the clown has gone and expresses concern for the loss of her handkerchief. If Othello were the jealous type, Desdemona says, she would worry more, since he might resort to ''ill thinking.'' However, Desdemona is certain that ''the sun where he was born/Drew all such humours from him.''
Othello enters and takes Desdemona's hand:

This argues fruitfulness and liberal heart:
Hot, hot, and moist: this hand of yours requires
A sequester from liberty, fasting and prayer,
Much castigation, exercise devout;
For here's a young and sweating devil here,
That commonly rebels. 'Tis a good hand,
A frank one.

Othello then asks Desdemona for her handkerchief, the strawberry spotted one, which she says she is not carrying with her. ''That's a fault,'' Othello replies. He continues:

That handkerchief
Did an Egyptian to my mother give;
She was a charmer, and could almost read

The thoughts of people: she told her, while she
kept it
'Twould make her amiable and subdue my father
Entirely to her love, but if she lost it
Or made a gift of it, my father's eye
Should hold her loathed and his spirits should hunt
After new fancies: she dying gave it me,
And bid me, when my fate would have me wive,
To give it her. I did so: and take heed on 't;
Make it a darling like your precious eye;
To lose 't or give 't away were such perdition
As nothing else could match.
Desdemona: Is 't possible?

Othello: 'Tis true: there's magic in the web of it:
A sibyl, that had number'd in the world
The sun to course two hundred compasses,
In her prophetic fury sew'd the work;
The worms were hallow'd that did breed the silk;
And it was dyed in mummy which the skilful
Conserved of maidens' hearts.

Finally, after Othello questions Desdemona and demands to
see the handkerchief, she admits that it is lost. Othello leaves in a
rage, and Emilia comments:

'Tis not a year or two shows us a man:
They are all but stomachs and we all but food;
They eat us hungerly, and when they are full
They belch us.

Cassio and Iago enter now. Cassio again asks Desdemona to
speak to Othello on his behalf, but Desdemona explains that something "hath puddled his clear spirit." Nevertheless, she offers to
find Othello and speak to him about Cassio once again.

Cassio, left alone, is approached by Bianca, his mistress, who
scolds him for staying away from her too long. Cassio apologizes
and gives her Desdemona's handkerchief, explaining that he found
it in his room and that he would like her to copy the embroidery.
Bianca is jealous at first, but when Cassio denies her accusations,
she calms down and agrees to take the handkerchief.

ACT IV

Iago continues to poison Othello's mind against Desdemona and Cassio. Finally, Othello loses control of himself and falls in a trance. As he lies there, Iago exclaims:

Work on,
My medicine, work! Thus credulous fools are caught;
And many worthy and chaste dames even thus,
All guiltless, meet reproach.

Cassio returns unexpectedly, but Iago warns him to stay away, saying that he should return after Othello has recovered and left. When Othello awakens, though, Iago does not send him away, but suggests that he wait until Cassio returns and eavesdrop on the conversation. When Othello goes to hide, Iago, in an aside, reveals his scheme:

Now will I question Cassio of Bianca,
A housewife that by selling her desires
Buys herself bread and clothes: it is a creature
That dotes on Cassio; as 'tis the strumpet's plague
To beguile many and be beguiled by one.
He, when he hears of her, cannot refrain
From the excess of laughter. Here he comes.

Cassio returns, and Iago proceeds to draw Cassio into his trap. Hearing Cassio's disrespectful remarks about Bianca and supposing that they refer to Desdemona, Othello goes into a jealous rage.

Bianca enters at this point and begins to scold Cassio again about the handkerchief, which she calls "some minx's token." Cassio attempts to calm her, but she rushes off. Iago persuades Cassio to follow her.

Othello, now convinced that Desdemona gave Cassio the handkerchief, which he casually passed on to his mistress, comes out of hiding and says, "How shall I murder him, Iago?" Othello quickly decides to murder Desdemona also:

Ay, let her rot, and perish, and be damned to-night; for
she shall not live: no, my heart is turned to stone; I strike
it, and it hurts my hand. O, the world hath not a sweeter
creature: she might lie by an emperor's side, and command him tasks.

Othello asks Iago to get him poison, but Iago suggests a
different method of murdering her:

Do it not with poison, strangle her in her bed, even the
bed she hath contaminated.
Othello: Good, good: the justice of it pleases: very
good.
Iago: And for Cassio, let me be his undertaker: you
shall hear more by midnight.

Desdemona enters with Lodovico, who is carrying letters
from Venice for Othello. As Othello reads the letters, Lodovico
asks Iago about Cassio. Desdemona interrupts to explain that there
has been trouble between Othello and Cassio. Desdemona's innocent remarks enrage Othello, and he finally strikes her. Lodovico,
shocked, urges Othello to apologize to Desdemona, but the Moor
exclaims:

O devil, devil!
If that the earth could teem with woman's tears,
Each drop she falls would prove a crocodile.
Out of my sight!

After Desdemona has left, Othello calls her back and insults
her further, talking to Lodovico:

Sir, she can turn and turn, and yet go on,
And turn again; and she can weep, sir, weep;
And she's obedient, as you say, obedient,
Very obedient. Proceed you in your tears.
Concerning this, sir – O well-painted passion! –
I am commanded home. Get you away;
I'll send for you anon. Sir, I obey the mandate,
And will return to Venice. Hence, avaunt!

Othello then invites Lodovico to supper and leaves, muttering, ''Goats and monkeys!''

Lodovico, left alone with Iago, expresses his surprise at the change in Othello. Convinced that Othello is insane, Lodovico leaves to follow Othello and observe him.

Othello, meanwhile, has gone to find Desdemona and confront her about her wrongdoing. He speaks first to Emilia, who denies Othello's accusations against Desdemona and Cassio and condemns the ''wretch'' who has planted such thoughts in Othello's mind.

Othello orders Emilia to bring Desdemona to him. After sending Emilia out to guard the door, Othello turns to Desdemona and accuses her of being false to him. Desdemona pleads for an explanation of these charges, and Othello cries:

Was this fair paper, this most goodly book,
Made to write 'whore' upon? What committed!
Committed! O thou public commoner!
I should make very forges of my cheeks,
That would to cinders burn up modesty,
Did I but speak thy deeds. What committed!
Heaven stops the nose at it, and the moon winks;
The bawdy wind, that kisses all it meets,
Is hush'd within the hollow mine of earth,
And will not hear it. What committed!
Impudent strumpet!

Desdemona protests that she is not a ''strumpet,'' but Othello refuses to believe her. He calls Emilia, flings some money at her and leaves the two women alone.

Stunned by Othello's treatment of her, Desdemona answers Emilia's questions briefly and asks her to find Iago. When Iago enters, Desdemona and Emilia describe Othello's unjust treatment of his wife. Emilia angrily exclaims:

I will be hang'd, if some eternal villain,
Some busy and insinuating rogue,
Some cogging, cozening slave, to get some office,
Have not devised this slander; I'll be hang'd else.

Desdemona begs Iago to speak to Othello and convince him of

her faithfulness and undying love for her husband. Iago assures her
that "all things shall be well" and sends the women away.

As the women go out, Roderigo enters, very upset about the
many jewels he has so unsuccessfully sent through Iago as presents
to win Desdemona's love. Iago has said he has delivered them, but
nothing has come of it. Roderigo says that he is going to
Desdemona to get his jewels back. If she does not return them, he
tells Iago, "I will seek satisfaction of you."

Iago responds by assuring Roderigo that he will win
Desdemona. Iago then tells him that Cassio is supposed to take
Othello's place in Cyprus, while the Moor is to leave for
Mauritania with Desdemona. If Roderigo is daring enough to kill
Cassio, however, Othello and Desdemona will have to stay in
Cyprus, and Roderigo's hopes may be fulfilled. Iago's plan, of
course, is thus to get rid of both Cassio and Roderigo.

Meanwhile, Lodovico, Othello and Desdemona are talking.
Othello, before going for a walk with Lodovico, orders
Desdemona to go to bed at once and dismiss Emilia. Emilia prepares the bed, laying on it Desdemona's wedding sheets. As Emilia
assists her mistress, Desdemona sings a sad song about the willow
and a maid who was deserted. At the song's end, she is left alone to
wait for Othello.

ACT V

It is nighttime, and Iago and Roderigo wait in the dark for Cassio. As Cassio enters, Roderigo stabs him, but not fatally. Cassio manages to wound Roderigo, and Iago, from behind, stabs Cassio in the leg and rushes away.

Othello enters and, hearing Cassio's voice calling for aid, exclaims:

'Tis he. O brave Iago, honest and just,
That hast such noble sense of thy friend's wrong!
Thou teachest me. Minion, your dear lies dead,
And your unblest fate hies: strumpet, I come!
Forth of my heart those charms, thine eyes, are
blotted;
Thy bed lust-stain'd shall with lust's blood be spotted.

The noise has aroused Lodovico and his companion, Gratiano, who come to help as Iago appears with a light. Gradually, the three recognize one another through the darkness. But, as Cassio and Roderigo again cry out, Iago stabs Roderigo to quiet him, pretending that he is to blame for the disturbance. Finally, the noise attracts Bianca, and Iago immediately directs the attention of the others to her as the probable cause of the argument.

Meanwhile, in her bedchamber, Desdemona lies asleep with a light burning by her. Othello enters and speaks:

It is the cause, it is the cause, my soul:
Let me not name it to you, you chaste stars!
It is the cause. Yet I'll not shed her blood,
Nor scar that whiter skin of hers than snow
And smooth as monumental alabaster.
Yet she must die, else she'll betray more men.
Put out the light, and then put out the light:
If I quench thee, thou flaming minister,
I can again thy former light restore,
Should I repent me: but once put out thy light,
Thou cunning'st pattern of excelling nature,
I know not where is that Promethean heat
 That can thy light relume. When I have pluck'd the
rose,
I cannot give it vital growth again,
It must needs wither: I'll smell it on the tree.
                                    [Kissing her.]

Ah, balmy breath, that dost almost persuade
Justice to break her sword! One more, one more:
Be thus when thou art dead, and I will kill thee,
And love thee after: one more, and this the last:
So sweet was ne'er so fatal. I must weep,
But they are cruel tears: this sorrow's heavenly;
It strikes where it doth love. She wakes.

When Desdemona wakes up, Othello offers her an opportunity to pray before she dies. Desdemona is suddenly frightened, realizing that Othello intends to murder her, but she still cannot understand his motive. At last, Othello accuses her directly of giving his handkerchief to Cassio. She denies it and begs him to let Cassio confirm her words. But Othello tells her that he has seen Cassio with the handkerchief, that Cassio has confessed his love for Desdemona and that now "his mouth is stopp'd." Desdemona's cry of horror at the news of Cassio's death is interpreted by Othello as grief for her lover. In spite of her pleading for mercy, Othello smothers Desdemona.

Emilia calls from outside the door. Othello makes sure that Desdemona dies quickly and painlessly. He draws the curtains around Desdemona's bed and lets Emilia in.

Emilia brings news of Roderigo's murder. Othello, of course, expected to hear of Cassio's death:

Not Cassio kill'd! then murder's out of tune,
And sweet revenge grows harsh.

They are interrupted by a faint cry from Desdemona, who is not dead after all. She weakly protests her innocence. When Emilia asks, "Who hath done this deed," Desdemona, protecting her husband, replies:

Nobody; I myself. Farewell:
Commend me to my kind lord: O, farewell!
                                        [Dies.]

This lie, spoken to save Othello, only strengthens his belief in her deceit:

She's like a liar gone to burning hell:
'Twas I that kill'd her.

Emilia tells Othello, ''Thou art rash as fire,'' and Othello proceeds to explain the reasons for his actions:

Cassio did top her; ask thy husband else.
O, I were damn'd beneath all depth in hell,
But that I did proceed upon just grounds
To this extremity. Thy husband knew it all.

Horrified to learn that her husband is to blame for Othello's mistaken belief in Desdemona's infidelity, she cries:

If he say so, may his pernicious soul
Rot half a grain a day! he lies to the heart:
She was too fond of her most filthy bargain.

Her outcries are answered by Montano, Gratiano and Iago. Emilia immediately accuses her husband of villainy, and Iago acknowledges that he told Othello of Desdemona's involvement with Cassio. Iago tries to hush Emilia, but she defies him and condemns Othello.

Othello makes no attempt to escape the consequences of his crime. He tells Gratiano, Desdemona's uncle, why he killed her, and Gratiano responds:

Poor Desdemona! I am glad thy father's dead:
Thy match was mortal to him, and pure grief
Shore his old thread in twain: did he live now,
This sight would make him do a desperate turn,
Yea, curse his better angel from his side,
And fall to reprobation.

Emilia is about to reveal the whole truth. Iago threatens to stab her, but she manages to tell Othello:

O thou dull Moor! that handkerchief thou speak'st of
I found by fortune and did give my husband;
For often with a solemn earnestness,
More than indeed belong'd to such a trifle,
He begg'd of me to steal it.

Iago denies her story, but Othello, convinced, tries to attack

Iago. Iago stabs Emilia and runs away. Montano rushes off after
Iago, and Gratiano stays by the door to prevent Othello's escape.

Emilia, fatally wounded by Iago, lies by her mistress, sings
snatches of the willow song and dies protesting to Othello that
Desdemona was always true to him.

Othello, meanwhile, discovers a sword in the room. Pretending that he is unarmed, Othello asks Gratiano to let him out of the
room or to come in and speak with him.

But, when Gratiano enters, Othello shows him the weapon
and says:

> Behold, I have a weapon;
> A better never did itself sustain
> Upon a soldier's thigh: I have seen the day
> That with this little arm and this good sword
> I have made my way through more impediments
> Than twenty times your stop: but, O vain boast!
> Who can control his fate? 'tis not so now.
> Be not afraid, though you do see me weapon'd;
> Here is my journey's end, here is my butt
> And very sea-mark of my utmost sail.
> Do you go back dismay'd? 'tis a lost fear:
> Man but a rush against Othello's breast,
> And he retires. Where should Othello go?
> Now, how dost thou look now? O ill-starr'd wench!
> Pale as thy smock! when we shall meet at compt,
> This look of thine will hurl my soul from heaven,
> And fiends will snatch at it. Cold, cold, my girl!
> Even like thy chastity. O cursed slave!
> Whip me, ye devils,
> From the possession of this heavenly sight!
> Blow me about in winds! roast me in sulphur!
> Wash me in steep-down gulfs of liquid fire!
> O Desdemona! Desdemona! dead!
> Oh! Oh! Oh!

The rest of the company returns with Iago as prisoner and
Cassio, carried in a chair. Othello wounds Iago with his Spanish
sword. He asks Cassio's pardon for what he has done and begs him
to ask Iago why he has ruined him. But Iago refuses to speak:
''From this time forth I never will speak a word.'' Othello's only

justification for his actions is his belief that he was satisfying his honor in murdering Desdemona: "For nought I did in hate, but all in honour."

Lodovico explains the whole matter by producing a letter, found in Roderigo's pocket, that tells how Roderigo was to kill Cassio. A second letter, written by Roderigo to Iago but never sent, is filled with complaints against Iago. Evidently, Iago had succeeded in winning him over again before it could be sent to him.

Cassio adds to the story by explaining that he had found the handkerchief in his room, where Iago had confessed to dropping it. He goes on to say that Roderigo's letter also told how Iago had persuaded Roderigo to start the quarrel that led to Cassio's dismissal.

Lodovico tells Othello that he must lose his command, while Cassio is to become governor of Cyprus. Othello will be kept prisoner until the state of Venice decides his fate. Iago is to be treated as he deserves: "if there be any cunning cruelty/That can torment him much and hold him long,/It shall be his."

Othello asks to be allowed to speak before they go:

Soft you; a word or two before you go.
I have done the state some service, and they know't.
No more of that. I pray you, in your letters,
When you shall these unlucky deeds relate,
Speak of me as I am; nothing extenuate,
Nor set down aught in malice: then must you speak
Of one that loved not wisely but too well;
Of one not easily jealous, but, being wrought,
Perplex'd in the extreme; of one whose hand,
Like the base Indian, threw a pearl away
Richer than all his tribe; of one whose subdued eyes,
Albeit unused to the melting mood,
Drop tears as fast as the Arabian trees
Their medicinal gum. Set you down this;
And say besides, that in Aleppo once,
Where a malignant and a turban'd Turk
Beat a Venetian and traduced the state,
I took by the throat the circumcised dog
And smote him, thus.

[Stabs himself.]

Lodovico closes the play with a speech condemning Iago and assigning Othello's possessions to Gratiano:

O Spartan dog,
More fell than anguish, hunger, or the sea!
Look on the tragic loading of this bed;
This is thy work: the object poisons sight;
Let it be hid. Gratiano, keep the house,
And seize upon the fortunes of the Moor,
For they succeed on you. To you, lord governor,
Remains the censure of this hellish villain,
The time, the place, the torture:
O, enforce it!
Myself will straight aboard, and to the state
This heavy act with heavy heart relate.

Part B:
Questions and Answers by Act and Scene

ACT I • SCENE 1

Question 1.
Why does the play open with a scene in which Othello himself does not appear?

Answer
By showing the forces that are to work against Othello, the first scene creates an atmosphere of suspense and dread that prepares the audience for his appearance later. The romance of his elopement also surrounds him with mystery and interest.

Question 2.
What is Iago's complaint against Othello?

Answer
Othello has chosen as his lieutenant Michael Cassio, a Florentine, more skilled, according to Iago, in the theory than in the practice and experience of war. Iago has been given the inferior position of Othello's ancient, his ensign or personal attendant.

Question 3.
What sort of men does Iago scorn and admire?

Answer
He despises those who carry out their duty faithfully and receive no reward: ''Whip me such honest knaves.'' He admires those who outwardly are loyal to their employers but privately are looking after their own interests: ''These fellows have some soul;/ And such a one do I profess myself.''

Question 4.
How does Iago justify his deceit in pretending friendship toward Othello?

Answer
He confesses that the national emergency of the Turkish wars

makes Othello's services valuable to Venice. Iago also knows that he must put on a show of faithfulness toward his general to gain success for himself.

Question 5.

Why does Shakespeare introduce Othello through hostile eyes?

Answer

At least two things are accomplished by this method of opening the play. We are aware, from the beginning, of Iago's true nature. We are also immediately aware that, in his opinion of Iago, at least, Othello is deceived. Our first impression of Othello, when he does appear, is enhanced—we find him to be nobler than we had expected. At the same time, however, this impression of greatness carries with it some doubt regarding the continuation of that greatness, since he accepts Iago at face value.

Question 6.

Describe and account for Brabantio's reaction to his daughter's elopement.

Answer

Brabantio is upset and angry to learn that his daughter has sneaked off to marry Othello without his permission and approval. Brabantio's position is understandable here; he should not be regarded as a comic type. According to the customs of the times, a woman of noble family was expected to receive her father's permission for marriage. Indeed, the marriage was usually arranged by the father and mother, often without the daughter's consent (see *Romeo and Juliet*). As a noblewoman, Desdemona was also expected to marry into a noble Venetian family. Since she has ignored the customs of her kind, she naturally angers her father. The audience is expected to understand Brabantio's feelings here and note his daughter's disobedience.

Question 7.

What impression do we get of Roderigo's character in this scene?

Answer

He is a young Venetian gentleman, who is foolish, naïve and

not very bright. He is easily led and falls under Iago's dominance quickly and totally. Roderigo has no mind of his own; he is easily fooled and lacks maturity and common sense.

<h1 style="text-align:center">ACT I • SCENE 2</h1>

Question 1.

How are Othello's calmness and confidence revealed in this scene?

Answer

He answers Iago's false regret at having resisted attacking Roderigo for his insults against the general by '' 'Tis better thus.'' In spite of Iago's attempts to alarm him over Brabantio's anger and influence, he replies, ''Let him do his spite'' and goes on to give his reasons for his assurance. He refuses to leave when it is evident that the searchers are approaching. ''You were best go in,'' says Iago, and Othello replies, ''Not I; I must be found./My parts, my title, and my perfect soul/Shall manifest me rightly.'' When there seems danger of violence between his party and that of Brabantio, he is calm, even poetic: ''Keep up your bright swords, for the dew will rust them.'' He refuses to be shaken by Brabantio's threats of prison and confidently points out that the Duke's business with him is more important than Brabantio's private complaints.

Question 2.

What does this scene accomplish in terms of plot development?

Answer

The scene manages to advance the plot significantly. The idea of having the senate called together over pressing matters in Cyprus at the same time that Brabantio and his men are out searching for Othello leads to a confrontation in the street. Furthermore, Iago's opening lines to Othello — that he would have struck Brabantio for making cruel remarks about Othello, except for his moral concern — establish his essential hypocrisy and evil more openly. Othello's few lines are not that revealing, but this is why they are significant: as a man of action and a good soldier, Othello should not be making lengthy speeches in the street to his aide, Iago. Iago's quick pretence of fighting with Roderigo reveals to us how cunning Iago can be on the spur of the moment. Iago also makes good use of one brief second alone with Cassio to begin to tell him about Othello's secret marriage. Iago makes the most of every opportunity, a quality that enlarges our image of him as a schemer.

ACT I • SCENE 3

Question 1.

What is the news that the Duke and his council are considering at the beginning of this scene?

Answer

Three reports, differing as to the number of ships involved, state that a large number of Turkish vessels are heading toward the island of Cyprus. A later report states that the Turkish fleet is destined for the island of Rhodes. This seems unlikely, as Rhodes is less important than Cyprus. Finally, there is a message that the fleet has joined reinforcements off Rhodes and that the whole force is now on its way to Cyprus.

Question 2.

How does this news affect the course of the play?

Answer

In such an emergency, Othello is the one man to whom all turn for leadership. He must go to Cyprus to take charge. This great responsibility and high honor make his later downfall more spectacular.

Question 3.

Contrast the attitude of the Duke toward Desdemona's marriage before and after he knows that her husband is Othello.

Answer

Hearing only that she has been "corrupted by spells and medicines," he exclaims "Whoe're he be that in this foul proceeding/Hath thus beguiled your daughter of herself/And you of her, the bloody book of law/You [Brabantio] shall yourself read in the bitter letter/After you own sense, yea, though our proper son/Stood in your action." When he learns that Othello is the husband, the Duke at first shows regret, then gives the Moor an opportunity to explain matters: "What, in your own part, can you say to this?" He criticizes Brabantio for accusing Othello of witchcraft without proof: "To vouch this, is no proof." Upon hearing Othello's story, he remarks, "I think this tale would win my daughter too." He advises Brabantio to accept the fact and make the best of it. Finally, he dismisses them with the words, "And, noble signior,/If virtue no delighted beauty lack,/Your son-in-law is far more fair than black."

Question 4.

Why does the Duke speak in prose in lines 221–228?

Answer

Prose is used to emphasize the importance of the matters being discussed, to make a break between the emotional atmosphere of the preceding scene and to give a sense of urgency to his words.

Question 5.

How does this scene contribute to the characterizations of Othello and Desdemona?

Answer

This scene contains the first of a series of comments by other characters describing Othello's courage and ability as a warrior. The impression is further strengthened by Othello's conduct. To begin with, his answer to Brabantio's charge of witchcraft is admirably controlled, in contrast with Brabantio's hysteria. Othello's most appealing quality, his simplicity, is observable in this scene. He has been a soldier since he was seven years old. The life and customs of the soldier are what he is used to, and, to him, war is a proud and glorious way of life.

This scene also serves to develop the character of Desdemona. Desdemona, as her father says, is modest and shy. But he underestimates her strength of mind and has failed to notice the aggressive qualities in his daughter.

Question 6.

How does the tragic element of the play begin to take shape here?

Answer

This scene is particularly important because it contains many of the seeds of the tragedy yet to be unfolded. For example, Iago's reputation for good-hearted, soldierly honesty is a major reason behind his control over Othello later in the play. Othello has no reason to distrust Iago at this point. It is evident that Othello also trusts his wife, since he assigns her to the care of another man. The lack of a hint of jealousy here makes Othello's later breakdown more striking.

Question 7.

Describe Iago's relationship with Roderigo.

Answer

Iago is basically cynical, yet he can offer other people conventional advice on how to value themselves. Even the encouragement he offers to Roderigo involves a cynicism toward love for others. Roderigo is Iago's easiest victim, serving as a source of income and also as an assistant for his schemes. Roderigo is an Elizabethan ''gull'' — what we would call a sucker today. Iago scorns Roderigo's stupidity, but he is willing to make use of it.

ACT II • SCENE 1

Question 1.

Compare the treatment of time in this scene with that of the first act.

Answer

In the first act, the time that it would take to play the scenes corresponds more or less exactly to the time that is supposed to elapse. In the rest of the play, events are represented as happening at a speed that could not possibly be true in real life. For instance, in this scene, three ships presumably arrive and land their passengers and their cargo in a very short space of time. From his ship, Cassio has seen the destruction of practically the whole Turkish fleet, a disaster that must have taken more time than appears to have elapsed. This dramatic time, in which long periods are compressed into a short space of action on the stage, creates urgency, a sense of haste and approaching events.

Question 2.

How does Shakespeare bring out the difference in age between Othello and Desdemona?

Answer

When they meet, Othello is so full of happiness and content-
ment that he feels no greater joy can ever come to him: ''If it were
now to die,/'Twere now to be most happy . . .I fear,/My soul hath
her content so absolute/That not another comfort like to this/
Succeeds in unknown fate.'' This is the attitude of an older person,
one who knows that happy experiences cannot always hope to be
repeated. Desdemona, however, is young and looks toward the
future: ''The heavens forbid/But that our loves and comforts
should increase,/Even as our days do grow!''

Question 3.

What is the significance of the storm at the beginning of this
scene?

Answer

The storm has threatening suggestiveness and an almost
supernatural violence. This is a preview, in sailing terms, of the
struggle Othello will have on shore and of his strong character in
facing it. But the optimism about the ''pilot,'' unfortunately, does
not apply to the kind of guidance he will have in his most desperate
need.

Question 4.

How does Iago propose to use Roderigo in his schemes?

Answer

He persuades Roderigo that Desdemona and Cassio are in
love. Having aroused Roderigo's jealousy against Cassio, he
arranges for Roderigo to anger Cassio by creating a disturbance of
some kind. Cassio will presumably lose his temper and strike
Roderigo—an offence that Iago will use to stir up the inhabitants of
Cyprus against Cassio and have him dismissed. In this way, Iago,
pretending to further Roderigo's hopes, will have Cassio removed
without having to take an active part in the proceedings.

Question 5.

Comment on the imagery Othello uses when he greets
Desdemona.

Answer

When Othello makes his entrance, he can fully express his joy at the sight of Desdemona only through images of the sea that he knows so well. Note the difference between the passion of his sea imagery and the flatness of Iago's. The speech is important also as pointing to the reunion and calm that usually follow a storm in Shakespeare. Here, there is irony, for the reunion and calm will be short. This passage also shows both the warmth and potential violence of Othello's love.

ACT II • SCENE 2

Question 1.
State the purpose of this scene.

Answer
This very brief scene establishes the action of the play in Cyprus. The war is over, and Othello is governor of the island and happily married. The coming celebrations, as the following scene will show, present Iago with the perfect opportunity to carry out his plans against Cassio.

ACT II • SCENE 3

Question 1.
What is the dramatic value of Cassio's brief question, "Where are they?"

Answer
This is Cassio's giving in to Iago's tempting. Until now, Cassio has held out against temptation. He knows that he has had quite enough to drink and that he is likely to do something foolish if he takes more. But Iago's persuasion is too strong, and Cassio gives in: "Where are these gallants who wish to drink a measure to Othello?"

Question 2.
How does Iago use Montano in this scene?

Answer
Pretending to feel great concern for Cassio, Iago cleverly manages to convince Montano that the lieutenant has a weakness

for drink, feeling sure that Montano will carry the tale to Othello. Montano is disturbed: ''It were well/The general were put in mind of it . . ./It were an honest action to say/So to the Moor.''

Question 3.

Usually, Iago's soliloquies occur at the end of a scene. Why does he indulge in quite a long one near the beginning of this scene?

Answer

This is the dramatist's way of allowing Cassio enough time to join the drinkers outside and, presumably, have a drink with them, for, when he enters again, he says: '' 'Fore God, they have given me a rouse already.''

Question 4.

Explain Iago's manipulation of people and circumstances here.

Answer

Throughout the play, Iago attempts to put his cynicism into action. Having assumed that Desdemona married Othello out of lust and that her tastes will change, he acts as though this theory were true. Having told Roderigo that Desdemona is attracted to Cassio — ''Didst thou not see her paddle with the palm of his hand?''– he again acts as though his wishes were facts.

Question 5.

Comment on the importance of reputation in the play.

Answer

Reputation is important in the play. Its loss deeply affects Cassio, who cries out: ''Oh God, that men should put an enemy in their mouths to steal away their brains!'' Cassio's downfall anticipates that of Othello, who also considers the public shame of Desdemona's infidelity and considers himself not an avenger but a judge. But, when Cassio cries, ''I have lost my reputation! I have lost the immortal part of myself, and what remains is bestial,'' the cynical Iago adds another of his mocking observations: ''Reputation is an idle and most false imposition, oft got without merit and lost without deserving. You have lost no reputation at all unless you repute yourself such a loser.'' In Cassio, reason is clouded by the wine Iago has urged upon him. The result is Cassio's violence, his loss of reputation and the chaos in his life — with order restored when Iago's villainy is revealed. In Othello, reason is clouded by Iago's cunning. The results for Othello are also violence, loss of reputation and the chaos in his life — with order tragically restored by his underlying nobility when Iago's villainy is revealed.

Question 6.

Discuss the passage of time in the play up until this point.

Answer

The difference between "stage time" and actual time may trouble careful readers. Within the space of the first scene of this act, three successive ships come into harbor and discharge their passengers. This scene starts in the evening, before the watch is due. Before it ends, Iago says "I must to the watch," but, without leaving, cries "By the mass, 'tis morning." Shakespeare's opinion of time may be caught in Iago's next words: "Pleasure and action make the hours seem short." Another swift passage of time is evident when Roderigo complains, "My money is almost spent," although the Venetians have just come to Cyprus, and his last act before sailing was to sell all his land.

Question 7.

How does Iago manage to sway people without arousing their suspicions?

Answer

Iago pretends that he does not want to offend anyone. When Montano tells Iago that Othello should be notified of Cassio's drunkenness, Iago's hypocritical answer is that he loves Cassio too much to get him in trouble with the general. He adds that he hopes Cassio will eventually be cured of this drinking vice. When Othello appears after the brawl Cassio has participated in and demands the truth, Iago is reluctant to speak. He appears not to wish to get anyone into trouble. He shows tolerance, consideration and discretion. This deception on Iago's part has a powerful effect on his listeners and always wins their admiration for his supposed discreetness. This trait also makes what he actually says more convincing because he seems to tell the truth reluctantly, but from the highest motives. Iago is finally "forced" to reveal the "truth" at

Othello's and Montano's urging, which makes his revelation even more convincing. Even then, he excuses Cassio and declares that Cassio must have had some good reason for his wild conduct. Othello's reaction is just the false impression Iago intended to create:

> I know, Iago,
> Thy honesty and love doth mince his position,
> Making it light to Cassio.

Cassio is dismissed from his position, and Iago, now pretending to be very concerned, can advise him to ask Desdemona to plead his cause.

Question 8.

Explain the significance of Iago's conversation with Cassio after Othello leaves.

Answer

The conversation between Iago and Cassio after Othello leaves offers both an insight into Cassio's character and an indication of Iago's mastery of psychology. The loss of reputation means more to Cassio than anything else, and he is perhaps overanxious in his efforts to regain Othello's favor. Iago's words to Cassio are ironic in the light of Iago's own reputation. They indicate how accomplished Iago is at saying what others would like to hear.

ACT III • SCENE 1

Question 1.

Is there any humor in this scene?

Answer

It has been said by some critics that there is no humor in Othello. Yet, before Cassio sees Emilia, there are approximately 28 lines of dialogue built primarily on the witty remarks of a clown. The clown, who is the jester or fool and apparently connected with Othello's followers, has several amusing lines that, for the moment, relieve the rather serious and somber movement of the play.

Question 2.

How is the villainy of Iago confirmed in this scene?

Answer

Again, we see how Iago can fool everyone by his false show of kindness and consideration. Cassio is completely taken in by Iago's pretended concern. If Iago is so able to fool all of the other characters, it is no wonder that his schemes succeed with Othello.

Question 3.

State the dramatic purpose of this scene.

Answer

This scene serves both as a kind of comic relief from the tension of the preceding scenes and as a breathing space for the audience before plunging into the highly emotional scenes that follow. The clown, like so many other Shakespearian jesters, is a master of the art of language and uses it cleverly to get laughs.

The end of the scene, when Cassio speaks to Emilia, is primarily intended to place Cassio where he may be seen parting from Desdemona in Scene 3 of this act.

ACT III • SCENE 2

Question 1.

What is the importance of this brief scene?

Answer

With Cassio's dismissal, Iago is now closer to Othello and will have more opportunity to work upon his feelings. Dramatically, the scene produces suspense by the knowledge that Othello and Iago are to meet later. Iago will use this meeting as a means of having Othello discover Cassio and Desdemona as they speak together.

ACT III • SCENE 3

Question 1.

Why is Cassio afraid that Othello will not take him back into his service unless Desdemona adds her pleadings?

Answer

Othello may consider it a matter of policy to keep Cassio in disgrace for some time. During that time, he may be satisfied with Cassio's replacement and forget his "love and service."

Question 2.

"Ha! I like not that!" To what does Iago refer in these words?

Answer

He is drawing attention to the fact that Cassio leaves as soon as Othello enters. Cassio does so merely because he is still ashamed and self-conscious about his foolish behavior the night before, but Iago makes it appear that Cassio does not want to be found talking with Desdemona.

Question 3.

How does Iago take advantage of Desdemona's words, "What! Michael Cassio,/That came a-wooing with you . . .?"

Answer

Iago suggests to Othello that, during the time that Cassio accompanied Othello to woo Desdemona, he had plenty of opportunity himself to win the lady's favor.

Question 4.

How does chance help Iago's plans in this scene?

Answer

It is by mere accident that Desdemona drops her handkerchief and that neither she nor Othello notices. Desdemona is concerned with Othello's headache; he is thinking of Iago's insinuations. By chance again, Emilia comes in to find it on the ground. Iago is quick to take advantage of the circumstance. He snatches the handkerchief from Emilia and plans to put it in Cassio's lodging, so that, sooner or later, Othello will see the lieutenant with it and draw the conclusion that Desdemona has given it to him.

Question 5.

What is the purpose of Othello's soliloquy in this scene?

Answer

The soliloquy in the crucial scene of the play shows us Othello after Iago's first attack. We see the poison already beginning to

48

work. But, more important, we see the conflict in Othello's mind between two opposing points of view—one condemns Desdemona; the other loves her. We see, too, the state of his mind. If his wife proves unfaithful, he'll "whistle her off, and let her down the wind/To prey at fortune."

Question 6.

What is the significance of Othello's farewell speech?

Answer

Othello says farewell not only to Desdemona but to his entire way of life. His speech echoes Cassio's earlier "Reputation, reputation, I have lost my reputation! I have lost the immortal part, sir, of myself, and what remains is bestial." It shows Othello aware of the action he is about to take and aware of the cost of that act, yet willing to sacrifice all for the sake of what is to him a higher law. This is the same Othello who takes his own life at the end, aware that his soul is condemned to hell.

Question 7.

Discuss the importance of this scene.

Answer

This scene, often called "the temptation scene," is perhaps the most important one in the entire play. In it, Iago plants the seeds of suspicion and jealousy that eventually bring about the tragic events of the drama. Ironically enough, it is Desdemona's attempt to restore peace between Othello and Cassio that gives Iago his first opportunity. She pleads Cassio's cause, arguing that Othello is doing himself a favor by taking Cassio back.

After she leaves, Iago begins weaving his web in what is possibly one of the most brilliant pieces of villainy in all Shakespeare. Step by step, he draws Othello into his net until the Moor is eaten up with jealousy. Some critics consider Othello too ready to seize upon an excuse for jealousy. There is, however, great power in Iago's sly hints. They strike at Othello's inability to deal with ambiguities, subtle suggestions and disorders.

ACT III • SCENE 4

Question 1.

What passages in this scene are examples of dramatic irony?

Answer

Desdemona tells the clown "I have moved my lord on his [Cassio's] behalf, and hope all will be well." Actually, all is far from well. Again, she assures Emilia that Othello is not jealous: "my noble Moor/Is true of mind and made of no such baseness/As jealous creatures are . . .I think the sun where he was born/Drew all such humours from him." She is sure that she understands his unkindness and blames it on matters of state: "Something, sure, of state . . .." She goes on to condemn herself for her lack of sympathy. Again, she repeats her confidence in Othello's freedom from jealousy: "Heaven keep that monster from Othello's mind!"

Question 2.

Already, Iago's influence is beginning to change Othello's nature, so that he resorts to deception instead of his usual frank and open nature. Give examples of this tendency in this scene.

Answer

Instead of confronting Desdemona with the rumors he has heard, Othello pretends that his feelings have not changed, although he finds it difficult to do so: "O, hardness to dissemble!" He holds her hand as if with affection, but, in reality, he finds its responsiveness a sign of her impulsive nature. He speaks in riddles — "Our new heraldry is hands, not hearts" — implying that Desdemona has given him her hand without giving him her heart. He pretends that he needs a handkerchief to wipe his eyes to find out whether she will confess her loss. The history of the handkerchief he relates is elaborate and probably contains some details that come from his own imagination, in order to impress Desdemona with the seriousness of losing this keepsake.

Question 3.

What changes are becoming noticeable in Othello?

Answer

Othello's language begins to change. He calls Desdemona "chuck," a word of affection, but on a lower level of familiarity. Later, his words and images approach the vulgar animal terms that are Iago's stock phrases. As he accepts Iago's lies, Othello sees through Iago's eyes and almost begins to speak through Iago's mouth.

Question 4.

How does the Elizabethan notion of the humours enter into this scene?

Answer

The Elizabethans often characterized people in terms of the ''humours,'' fluids of the body that were supposed to determine a man's temperament and disposition. Ben Jonson had just written two plays about man ''in his humour'' and ''out of his humour.'' The ''melancholy Jaques'' in *As You Like It* represents a common Elizabethan type. The ''four humours'' are the blood, phlegm, choler (bile) and black bile (melancholy).

In this scene, when Emilia wonders whether Othello is jealous, Desdemona replies: ''Who, he? I think the sun where he was born/Drew all such humours from him.'' Immediately afterward, Othello enters, takes Desdemona's hand and, finding it ''hot, hot, and moist,'' at once speaks to her with bitter irony, for such a humid hand was supposed to show a lustful spirit.

ACT IV • SCENE 1

Question 1.

Explain what Othello means by saying, ''Nature would not invest herself in such shadowing passion without some instruction.''

Answer

Othello trembles and feels a fit or trance coming over him. His thoughts are confused. He feels sure that this reaction could not be produced in him by words alone. There must be some truth touching his very nature below his conscious mind that brings about this feeling of depression.

Question 2.

Explain Cassio's reply to Iago: ''The worser that you give me the addition/Whose want even kills me.''

Answer

Iago has sarcastically greeted Cassio as ''lieutenant,'' knowing that he is upset over the loss of that title. Cassio means, ''I am worse off because you greet me by that title, whose loss kills me.''

Question 3.

Describe the progress of Othello's anger in this scene.

Answer

The change of moods in Othello is swift and violent. When Iago makes his suggestion of Desdemona's infidelity as though he were trying to excuse her—: "to be naked with her friend in bed an hour or more, not meaning any harm"—Othello struggles with the thought of the fair and faithful wife he knows. But Iago bluntly says Cassio has boasted, "Lie with her? Lie on her!" Othello's passion makes him so upset that he faints. After Cassio and Bianca leave, Othello comes from his hiding place, from where he has seen Desdemona's handkerchief. His love and basic gentleness toward his wife break through again as he exclaims: "Oh, the world hath not a sweeter creature. She might lie by an emperor's side, and command him tasks.../And then, of so gentle a condition." Iago's reminder, "Aye, too gentle," moves him to a difficult decision: "Nay, that's certain. But yet the pity of it, Iago. O Iago, the pity of it, Iago!" He is now about to take action. When Iago suggests that Othello might spare Desdemona and let her go on doing as she wills, Othello breaks out: "I will chop her into messes. Cuckold me!" Completely overcome by Iago's cunning, he asks Iago to get him some poison, but he accepts as more appropriate Iago's suggestion to "strangle her in her bed, even the bed she hath contaminated." Now, even in the presence of the state's messenger, a kinsman to her father, Desdemona's mention of her concern for Cassio makes Othello strike her.

ACT IV • SCENE 2

Question 1.

To what extent do Othello's religious feelings enter his treatment of Desdemona?

Answer

He has sworn a solemn oath to punish her, in Act III, Scene 3, where he kneels with Iago—"Now, by yond marble heaven,/In the due reverence of a sacred vow/I here engage my words." Emilia's defence of her mistress has come too late, for he has already given this sacred pledge, and he is not convinced by Emilia's words. He is shocked by the fact that Desdemona can kneel and pray, in spite of her guilt. Although he is sure that she is guilty, he is not satisfied that she is wicked enough to be punished until she damns herself by swearing what he is sure is a false oath. By doing so, he believes, she gives her soul to the devil.

Question 2.

How does Iago take advantage of Roderigo's boldness in criticizing him?

Answer

Instead of taking offence, Iago pretends to admire Roderigo's courage: ''if thou hast that in thee indeed, which I have greater reason to believe now than ever, I mean purpose, courage, and valour, this night show it.'' With these flattering words, Iago begins to regain Roderigo's confidence once more, susceptible as Roderigo is to compliments, and persuades him to use this courage in one more scheme — the murder of Cassio.

Question 3.

How is Othello becoming increasingly alienated from those around him?

Answer

Othello has grown more and more isolated in his delusion and more and more dependent upon Iago alone. First, he dismisses his loyal lieutenant, Cassio. Then, through Lodovico, he alienates the senators of Venice by his cruel treatment of Desdemona. Now, by treating Desdemona as a whore and Emilia as a keeper of a whore-house, he turns Emilia against him and leaves Desdemona frightened and uncertain about him.

Question 4.

What do we learn about Emilia in this scene? Does Iago feel threatened by her?

Answer

In this scene, Shakespeare shows us that there is more to Emilia than meets the eye. Othello underestimates Emilia's shrewdness and sense of right—but so does her husband. When she concludes that Othello's jealousy was the result of the plotting of some villain, Iago swiftly denies this, indicating a rather human nervousness about the success of his plan—not any real alarm at the recognition of his true nature.

ACT IV • SCENE 3

Question 1.

How does Iago take advantage of opportunities in this scene?

Answer

Iago realizes that the deaths of Roderigo and Cassio will help his cause. In the confusion that follows Iago's wounding of Cassio, Iago takes the opportunity to eliminate Roderigo. Iago kills him so that he no longer has to worry about returning Roderigo's jewels. Iago's opportunism, which has been seen throughout the play, is once more apparent in this episode. With his cunning and evil resourcefulness, Iago takes advantage of every opportunity to further his plot. Not only do the other characters ''play into his hands,'' but chance and fortune favor him until the last scene of the drama.

Iago's resourcefulness is also seen in the use he makes of Bianca's appearance. He is quite willing to suggest that Cassio and Roderigo have argued over her. ''This is the fruit of whoring,'' Iago declares, attempting to bring further disgrace to Cassio. Iago's quick thinking is masterly; he can turn everything to his advantage.

Question 2.

Contrast the characters of Emilia and Desdemona.

Answer

Desdemona lacks worldly wisdom and cannot understand the lower passions — including jealousy. In contrast to Desdemona's purity, Emilia has a humorously worldly approach to life. She has observed enough of life to make some shrewd comments upon the ways of men. Yet, despite her cleverness, she is no female counterpart of her husband.

Question 3.

Comment on the significance of Desdemona's song.

54

Answer

Possibly the most effective dramatic touch in this scene is the "Willow Song," with its sense of approaching tragedy. It seems that Desdemona senses her doom when she sings this song.

ACT V • SCENE 1

Question 1.

What evidence is there that Iago is beginning to have some doubts about the complete success of his plans?

Answer

He says to Roderigo, while they wait to try to murder Cassio, "It makes us, or it mars us." Again, at the close of the scene, he allows a question to enter his mind: "This is the night/That either makes me or fordoes me quite."

Question 2.

What does Iago say that gives us an insight into the reasons why he performs evil deeds against people who have done him no wrong?

Answer

Speaking of Cassio, he says "He hath a daily beauty in his life/That makes me ugly." Although he despises those who are naturally good and behave with nobility, with no thought of reward, he still feels the difference between them and himself. He is incapable of appreciating their goodness, but he recognizes its presence and hates it because it is something entirely foreign to his own nature.

Question 3.

Comment on Othello's words:

Forth of my heart, those charms, thine eyes, are
blotted;
Thy bed, lust-stained, shall with lust's blood be
spotted.

Answer

There is a savagery in Othello's words here. This violence

contrasts sharply with his earlier sorrow and with his anguish at being forced, as he sees it, to an act not of vengeance but of retribution to clear his honor.

Yet his love for Desdemona is so strong that he might not have overcome it and wiped out his shame by her death had not a fierce desire for vengeance swept him along. This wild fever of revenge surges through him when he thinks the "brave Iago, honest and just," has killed his wife's lover. His nature is a mixture of pride and passion.

ACT V • SCENE 2

Question 1.
Explain lines 63–65, beginning "O perjur'd woman . . . ."

Answer
Othello's decision to kill Desdemona is based upon his religious beliefs: the murder is to be a sacrifice, not a deed of revenge. When she persists in swearing to what Othello believes to be a falsehood, he fears that she will harden his heart and transform the sacrifice into an act of vengefulness.

Question 2.
Explain the superstition referred to in lines 284–287: "I look down towards his feet . . . ."

Answer
The devil is supposed to have cloven feet, like a goat or similar animal. Othello looks down at Iago's feet to see if he shows this diabolic sign, and then he discards the idea — "but that's a fable." Iago continues the simile: "I bleed, sir; but not kill'd," implying that he is a devil and so cannot die.

Question 3.
Explain the opening words of this scene.

Answer
The opening words of the final scene are pathetic. Coming into the room where Desdemona is sleeping, Othello says to himself, "It is the cause, it is the cause, my soul." The word, "cause," is a legal term. But Othello's court has already reached a

verdict. Selfless spiritual concern and self-centered violence are confused. Othello, acting as judge, priest and executioner, is serving the law of his own passion.

Question 4.

Comment on the inconsistent explanations of the origins of Desdemona's handkerchief.

Answer

Subtleties in Shakespeare may be significant; not every inconsistency is a careless mistake. In this scene, saying that he saw Desdemona's handkerchief in Cassio's hand, Othello calls it "an antique token/My father gave my mother." To Desdemona, he had emphasized that an Egyptian, who was a "charmer" and had set a spell of true love on its owner, had given it to his mother. Is this a slip of Shakespeare's or a further instance of his art? Othello tells the story to Desdemona to make her feel the value of his token, which she must not lose or give to another man. This slight departure from truth, this story to lend emphasis, works to the fatal end. If Othello had not overexcited Desdemona's fears by his story, she might have told him, honestly and directly, that she had lost the handkerchief and thus taken much of the poison from Iago's sting.

Question 5.

How does the element of surprise enter into the final scene?

Answer

The final scene of *Othello* marks one of Shakespeare's infrequent uses of surprise. Surprise is common in the trivial farce and in the detective melodrama. Good plays generally rely upon suspense, which means poised expectancy, waiting to see not so much what the end will be as how it will be brought about. They also rely upon dramatic irony, when the audience knows what the characters do not. But there is genuine surprise at the end of Othello's speech of redemption, before he stabs himself. Some actors have him approach Iago (whom he has already attacked and wounded) so that his sudden suicide is still more startling.

Question 6.

What noble trait do both Desdemona and Othello reveal before their deaths?

Answer

Note that the dying Desdemona takes on herself the blame for her death. Even then, she cannot accuse Othello. Similarly, Othello's last words are on a high level of dignified and honest awareness of his guilt and responsibility.

Question 7.

How does Othello regard the murder of Desdemona?

Answer

Othello regards his killing of Desdemona as a sort of sacrifice. He is a judge punishing a woman who has betrayed a man and might betray more men in the future: "She must die, else she'll betray more men." He regards himself as the hand of justice. He commits the murder not "in hate, but all in honour."

Question 8.

How is Othello's greatness emphasized in this scene?

Answer

Lodovico testifies to Othello's greatness and his present state of deterioration:

O thou Othello, that were once so good,
Fall'n in the practice of a damned slave."

In this condition, Othello cannot live. His sorrow and regret are too great for life. He feels the only honorable thing to do is to join Desdemona in death. Cassio remarks that he feared a suicide by Othello under these circumstances because "he was great of heart."

Question 9.

Does Iago account for the motives behind his villainy?

Answer

Iago confesses part of his villainy, but he does not reveal the motives that prompted him to vengeance. To have Iago state his reasons at this point would be anticlimactic, and his silence seems to heighten the blackness of his character.

Question 10.

How does Othello picture his death?

Answer

In recognizing his total disgrace, Othello sees it all as the end of a sea voyage. Both the storm and the icy currents, with their beautiful yet terrible turbulence, are now gone. In the final kiss, Othello and Desdemona are reunited at last.

Part C:
General Review Questions and Answers

Question 1.

Describe the development of Othello's jealousy as it relates to the structure of the play.

Answer

Othello builds around the rising jealousy that Othello feels as the play progresses. In Act II, a chance meeting between Cassio and Desdemona reinforces Iago's idea of developing a jealous suspicion of the two in Othello's mind. Throughout Act III, Iago provokes Othello's jealousy, and the Moor becomes more and more certain that there really is a romance between his wife and Cassio. When Iago arranges to obtain Desdemona's handkerchief and have Cassio seen with it, the play reaches a turning point. From the moment he sees the handkerchief, Othello is convinced of his wife's guilt. Othello is strengthened even further in his conviction when (also in Act IV) Lodovico brings news that Cassio is to replace Othello as commander in Cyprus. Othello's blind jealousy leads him to kill Desdemona. When he discovers her innocence too late, in the end, he kills himself. The play thus moves as Othello's jealousy dictates.

Iago's motivation for provoking Othello is provided early in the play when Cassio, rather than Iago, wins Othello's favor. This may be called the exciting action. The rising action that follows adds to Othello's doubts and jealousy. The climax arrives when Othello sees the handkerchief that he had given to Desdemona in the hands of Cassio's mistress, Bianca. The falling action then follows as Othello rapidly grows more depressed, and events progress swiftly to his killing of Desdemona and to his own suicide upon realizing her innocence. The play, in other words, depicts the planting of the seeds of jealousy, the growing of jealous feelings and the result of those feelings in the various murders in the end. There is exposition, conflict and catastrophe, for the structure is completely dependent upon the jealousy of Othello, which, in its growth and horror, leads to disaster. The plot explains the logic of the developing jealousy, while the structure of the play demonstrates it.

Question 2.

How does Shakespeare connect the various parts of the play?

Answer

Any play is automatically given a physical division into parts through the separation into acts and the scenes within each of those acts. But the connections between those acts and scenes are not automatic. Shakespeare had to develop a logical sequence of actions growing naturally out of the characters and the relationships between them. *Othello* moves smoothly and evenly from the early preparations for the tragedy, through a climax to its conclusion in disaster. The play has various turning points, each of which serves as a link to what will come. The first turning point comes at the beginning of the play when Iago announces his desire to destroy Othello. Previously, Iago has been Othello's good friend. But now, with the appointment of Cassio as Othello's lieutenant, Iago turns away from Othello and plots his downfall. This turning point leads logically and directly to other events of Act I, such as Iago's use of Roderigo to inform Brabantio that Othello has eloped with Desdemona.

Before we go on to the next turning point, we should notice the extremely delicate way in which Shakespeare establishes certain ideas and phrases that can later be repeated to bind the parts of the play together. In Act I, Scene 3, Brabantio says to Othello: "Look to her, Moor, if thou hast eyes to see:/She has deceived her father, and may thee." Later, in Act III, Scene 3, Iago uses the same point to further Othello's jealousy ("She did deceive her father, marrying you," etc.). Thus, Shakespeare has carefully introduced an idea early in the play that can be used as a unifying device later on.

In Act II, there is a chance meeting between Cassio and Desdemona that strengthens Iago's scheme of building a case against them. Then, Iago has Roderigo pick a fight with Cassio, who has been drinking. Iago summons Othello, who, in annoyance, reduces Cassio's rank. Iago can now suggest to Cassio that he ask Desdemona to speak to Othello and ask that he be reinstated as lieutenant. Shakespeare has manipulated the plot by having Iago determine the series of events. To make the Moor jealous, it was necessary for him to see Desdemona and Cassio together. By having Cassio seek Desdemona's help and by having her act in the interest of Cassio, Shakespeare not only provides a logical sequence of ideas and actions, but blends in a certain kind of irony that makes Othello's jealousy very unattractive.

Throughout the play, there is this kind of cause-and-effect structural development. The chance meeting between Desdemona and Cassio leads to Iago's scheme, which leads to Cassio's punishment, which leads to his private talks with Desdemona, which lead to Othello's increasing jealousy, which leads to his eventual murder of Desdemona and his own suicide, becoming a series of connected parts. By having a logical sequence of actions and by explaining those actions in terms of consistency of character action, Shakespeare's structure becomes automatic. There is no problem moving from Iago's revenge motives to the long middle section of the play, in which Othello's jealousy grows rapidly. Nor is there any difficulty in moving from this section to the final section of multiple murders. The structure of preparation, fall and aftermath becomes more than convenient; it provides excitement. We can almost sense in Act I the horrible conclusions that are going to arrive in Act V. The links between the parts of the play, when we move from one section to the next, as well as when we move from one act to the next, all succeed because of their tightly unified logic. The characters behave in ways that we consider logical and consistent with their patterns of thinking. The scheming Iago, the envious Roderigo, the loyal and good Cassio, the fair Desdemona and the ignorant Othello all perform their parts in a way that allows the events to grow out of one another into an unbroken logical chain that ends in death.

Question 3.

What is the relationship between conflict and structure in *Othello*?

Answer

In many Shakespearian tragedies, the conflict begins relatively early in the play. There is a constant alternation of advantage between the opposing forces. The structure of *Othello*, as many Shakespearian critics have noticed, is somewhat different. In *Othello*, the central conflict — Othello's raging sexual jealousy — is not really worked into the drama until the middle. There is an unusually long exposition and a delayed introduction of the conflict itself.

There is a great deal of preparation in Acts I and II, whereby Iago plots the ways in which Othello will first be made aware of a possible relationship between Desdemona and Cassio. But the actual conflict, the real agony, does not begin until the middle of the play, in Act III, where it gathers force when Othello sees the

62

so-called ''proof'' of Desdemona's guilt in the handkerchief. Once the conflict has been introduced, it grows extremely rapidly and leads almost in a straight line to Desdemona's death in Act V.

Instead of having the conflict introduced at an early point in the play, we have the conflict introduced in the middle, and, instead of showing an alternation of forces, the force of Othello's anger begins late and grows steadily until the end. The structure of the play is designed somewhat differently, in order to have a developing anger ''take over'' the entire play. There is little relief between Othello's discovery of guilt and the end of the play, whereas in the first few acts we find occasional scenes or sections of relief, provided by some humor or when men are discussing the Turks' intended invasion of Cyprus. In the second half of the play, Othello's private, raging passion dominates everything. The rather lengthy preparations for this jealousy, undertaken by Iago in the first two acts, thus lead only gradually into something violent and explosive.

In a way, the structure of *Othello* resembles a fuse and a powder keg, where the lighted fuse burns along slowly and evenly at first and then suddenly ignites the powder. There is not even a suggestion in the early parts of the play that Othello is capable of such anger, except for the assumption that he has always been a tough and brave military man. But, even in this dimension of his personality, the times when he barely escaped from danger are emphasized, not the times when he himself posed a threat of danger to someone else. Shakespeare has carefully postponed certain characteristics of Othello to a point in the developing structure where those characteristics would have the greatest impact on the audience. The conflict becomes enlarged in its being delayed, and, thus, the structure of the play is designed to magnify that conflict.

Question 4.

Discuss the development of Othello as a character.

Answer

Othello changes, but he does not develop, at least not until the end of the play, when he feels profound regret over his unjustified deed and displays a sincere and tender love for his murdered wife. This is the sensitive and loving Othello, whose positive side has been hidden most of the time.

Othello is a Moor, one that Shakespeare has deliberately made a black as well. He is a renowned military leader, a great soldier and one of the strong defending arms in the service of the state. He is a man who, through military training, perhaps, has learned to think in absolutes and to make quick decisions. His survival has often depended on quick action rather than on lengthy or studied considerations. He is a lonely man in the sense that he is a Moor among Venetian senators. He has been the guest of Brabantio and white society and, although proud of his heritage, realizes that he is, to a certain extent, alone. Desdemona has fallen in love with him primarily because of his bravery and for the dangers he has survived. As Othello explains to his accusers in Act I, Scene 3:

> My story being done,
> She gave me for my pains a world of sighs:
> She swore, in faith, 'twas strange, 'twas passing
> strange,
> 'Twas pitiful, 'twas wondrous pitiful: . . .
> She loved me for the dangers I had pass'd,
> And I loved her that she did pity them.
> This only is the witchcraft I have used.

In other words, Othello appealed to Desdemona's imagination and to her attraction to physical courage. This is the basic picture of Othello: the successful warrior, more a man of action than an intellectual, more a doer than a thinker.

This picture of the soldier is strengthened when we first see Othello placed in command of Cyprus and, then, in his joyful announcement that the Turks have been caught in a storm and will not attack. When Iago begins to make Othello jealous in the crucial third scene of the third act, we sense Othello's rapid suffering. Once he decides that Desdemona is unfaithful, Othello will hold on to that decision. At the same time, however, he will not make such a decision on little evidence:

> Think'st thou I'd made a life of jealousy,
> To follow still the changes of the moon
> With fresh suspicions? No; to be once in doubt
> Is once to be resolved.

Once he does have a real doubt, he will work to resolve that doubt immediately — no matter what this involves or what consequences may follow.

When Othello has slapped Desdemona in the face and called her a whore in front of Lodovico and the party from Venice, Lodovico asks:

> Is this the noble Moor whom our full senate
> Call all in all sufficient? Is this the nature
> Whom passion could not shake? Whose solid virtue
> The shot of accident, nor dart of chance,
> Could neither graze nor pierce?

Iago immediately replies with an understatement, simply saying that Othello has "changed." The point is that certain human emotions in Othello have just recently been brought to the surface. Othello may have "changed" as Iago suggests, but he has not "developed" in the sense of having become any more complex. He is still basically a simple character. His striking out at Desdemona is example enough that he still thinks in terms of rash physical violence and retribution.

Othello's jealousy does make him increasingly weak. When he has the proof of the handkerchief, he decides that Desdemona is unfaithful. Once he knows this, he also knows that he will punish her — swiftly and physically. As the play moves toward Desdemona's murder, Othello is not developing, but rather is becoming increasingly jealous and hateful. He moves like a frustrated animal and a weary soldier to the end, when he is at last broken down and moved by sorrow and tenderness. He has operated on an animal level instead of a complicated, intellectual level throughout the play.

Question 5.

To what extent is Iago a thematic character, representing evil for evil's sake?

Answer

A valid argument can be made that Iago is purely a thematic character, the personification of the force of evil that leads to the destruction of Othello and Desdemona. Many critics have demonstrated the pointlessness of explaining Iago's hatred of Othello. In the source of the play, Cinthio's novel, Iago is in love with

Desdemona, which becomes a major motive for his working for the downfall of Desdemona's husband. But Shakespeare has deliberately changed this story. Iago's love for Desdemona is mentioned only once, in his soliloquy at the end of Act II, Scene 1:

> The Moor, howbeit that I endure him not,
> Is of a constant, loving, noble nature:
> And I dare think he'll prove to Desdemona
> A most dear husband. Now, I do love her too;
> Not out of absolute lust, though peradventure
> I stand accountant for as great a sin . . .

Shakespeare makes no further reference to any love that Iago may feel for Desdemona, although, in the erotic lie that Iago describes as Cassio's dreaming of Desdemona to Othello, we see the evidence of what is perhaps Iago's own lust.

For the most part, then, Iago has little motivation for his behavior. The fact of Cassio's appointment to lieutenant receives scant discussion after the opening of the play. When Iago steps forward in soliloquies and describes his forthcoming evil acts, we begin to suspect that he does, indeed, have what Coleridge termed a "motiveless malignancy." We continually see the image of Iago as an evil spider trapping the innocent and helpless fly. For example, in Act II, Scene 1, upon seeing Desdemona touch Cassio's palm, Iago brags, "With as little a web as this will I ensnare as great a fly as Cassio." In the next major scene, referring to his plan of having Desdemona plead for Cassio to Othello, Iago confides:

> So will I turn her virtue into pitch,
> And out of her own goodness make the net
> That shall enmesh them all.

Iago enjoys his evil acts too much for them to require motives. Everything he does or says works directly toward the central conflict of the play.

Like Othello, Iago is not a developing character. He remains loyal to his ideal — or anti-ideal — of spiteful revenge. He is confident from the start of his ability to make Desdemona look guilty, even though he does not know how he will do it. After Emilia has found the handkerchief, she recalls that Iago often asked her to get it for him. In other words, Iago has been thinking of such a scheme all along. The use of the handkerchief is not a complete accident: it is, we suspect, one of several possibilities imagined by Iago. Iago is a scheming, yet fascinating, character, and to say that he is only a thematic character seems to strip him of certain human characteristics that emerge in the extreme enjoyment of his evil acts, his logical development of a foundation to support Othello's aroused jealous suspicions and his conversation with Emilia. After all, most purely evil characters are not even married. Shakespeare has chosen to give Iago a wife—one who is frankly realistic, as is seen in her discussion of unfaithfulness with Desdemona. Although we notice then that Iago is placed in a human position – that of husband and soldier – we still must conclude that he is primarily a character who creates evil for the sake of creating evil. When Emilia discovers that Iago is behind Othello's false suspicions, and the murder of Desdemona, she emphasizes Iago's essential villainy:

> Villainy, villainy, villainy!
> I think upon't, I think: I smell't: O villainy!
> I thought so then, I'll kill myself for grief:
> O villainy, villainy!

Iago is placed in the play for the explicit purpose of being the villain; evil is his reason for being. He has rightly been termed "the arch-criminal of Shakespearean drama."

Question 6.
Briefly contrast Desdemona and Emilia.

Answer
With the exception of Bianca, Cassio's mistress, who has very little to say, Desdemona and Emilia are the only women in the play. In Desdemona and Emilia, Shakespeare has presented a striking contrast between innocence and experience or between idealism and realism. Desdemona is a sweet, unsuspecting creature. Even as she slowly comes to realize that Othello plans to kill her, she acts normally. When he enters her bedchamber to murder her, she simply and calmly asks him to come to bed—even though she has had her wedding sheets placed on the bed, hinted to Emilia that she fears some disaster ahead and sung a song that her

mother's maid sang before her own death. Desdemona, in other words, is faithful to her love. She fell in love with Othello for what many of us would consider the wrong reasons, but nevertheless she is constant in that love. Even when Othello has cruelly slapped her, she refuses to lose her composure.

Emilia, on the other hand, as the wife of Iago, is expectedly hardened. She is a woman of the world, who makes no pretence of innocence and even suggests openly that she would allow her appetites to lead into adultery. Emilia is able to serve Desdemona loyally. In fact, she loves Desdemona very much, as is seen clearly in the last act of the play. Like any woman, she wants her husband's approval – which is why she is willing to give Iago the handkerchief – and in this one respect she has something in common with Desdemona. Emilia is coarse and aggressive. However, she remains relatively quiet until the last act, when she openly condemns Othello for killing Desdemona and fearlessly calls the alarm. While Emilia has no understanding of Desdemona's blind faithfulness and innocence, she is able to defend it before Othello at the end of the play. Her own husband has not made her happy, and yet she is relatively loyal to him until she discovers his major harmful act.

The contrast between Desdemona and Emilia is designed primarily to heighten our awareness of Desdemona's innocence and incredible loyalty to Othello. Emilia is in the play – as is Bianca – to show us that common women are coarse, fickle and lustful. Desdemona is the exception, of course, and, in the contrast, she acquires even greater nobility, becoming the bright moral light of the play. At the same time, however, Emilia is no harlot like Bianca, and she bravely defies her husband in order to see justice done at the end of the play.

Question 7.

Discuss Othello's opinion of Iago. Why is Othello fooled so easily?

Answer

Iago has been a professional soldier for a long time, and he is understandably annoyed when he sees Othello choose Cassio as his lieutenant. Why Othello chose Cassio instead of Iago is unknown and in some ways surprising, for Cassio does not have the confidence and experience of Iago. Othello's view of his "ancient," (that is, his underofficer) is that he is honest. In the opening of Act II, Scene 3, Othello tells Cassio to look after the men that night and keep peace. Cassio notes that Iago has been put in charge, and Othello replies, ''Iago is most honest.'' A little later, after the outbreak of violence, Othello asks Iago what has happened. Iago pretends that he does not want to speak against Cassio, but, in so doing, he makes Cassio look guilty. In other words, Othello is easily fooled — to the extent of being controlled — by Iago. Othello replies:

> I know, Iago,
> Thy honesty and love doth mince this matter,
> Making it light to Cassio. Cassio, I love thee;
> But never more be officer of mine.

Again, Othello refers to Iago's honesty. Iago, on the other hand, lies frequently when he says that he loves Othello very much. For example, when noting that Cassio has just left Desdemona (in Act III, Scene 3), Iago again pretends that he hates to tell Othello anything that might make him unhappy, but he maintains that he loves Othello too much to remain silent: ''I humbly do beseech you of your pardon/For too much loving you.'' Othello's reply is, ''I am bound to thee for ever,'' a statement that suggests the spider-fly relationship between Iago and Othello.

The entire relationship between Iago and Othello is basically static: Othello incorrectly thinks Iago is ''honest,'' while Iago lies and deceives Othello at every opportunity. The reason for this is that Othello himself is honest and unable to think of Iago as dishonest. It simply never occurs to him that someone who appears as honest as Iago could do him any harm. This is the same emotion experienced by Desdemona in her relationship to Othello, an ironic parallel. Only when Iago has strongly suggested that Desdemona and Cassio are secret lovers does Othello's manner of addressing Iago change: ''Villain, be sure thou prove my love a whore,/Be sure of it; give me the ocular proof.'' (Act III, Scene 3, 359–360).

Othello is easily fooled by Iago because Othello believes in appearances. This is one of the main points of the play: things are not always what they seem. Iago understands Othello's basic weakness, for he states clearly at the end of the first act:

> The Moor is of a free and open nature,

That thinks men honest that but seem to be so,
And will as tenderly be led by the nose
As asses are.

Iago knows not only that Othello is easily deceived by appearances, but also that Othello is convinced of Iago's honesty. This knowledge defines and determines the relationship between them. There is such a short time between Othello's discovery of Iago's deceit and the end of the play that it is pointless to discuss Othello's change or a change in the nature of the relationship.

Question 8.

Briefly describe Roderigo's motivation and his role within the play.

Answer

Roderigo is boyish, foolish and even at times unusually stupid, yet we never feel ourselves condemning him. This is explained partly by Roderigo's motivation: he is infatuated with Desdemona and has been for some time. He is willing to do anything to win her love, and the fact that she is so unattainable makes him that much more pathetic. He hands himself over to Iago at the beginning of the play, for he knows that he does not have the genius or the scheming power to win Desdemona. Roderigo has a certain amount of self-knowledge and an awareness of fundamental limitations that, from one point of view, puts him above some of the other characters in the play. In any case, Roderigo's honest and recognized love for Desdemona makes him at least acceptable in our eyes, and we feel sorry for him when he is so cruelly killed by Iago.

Roderigo has several functions in *Othello*. In the first place, it is necessary that the villain have some sort of helper or agent to assist in the execution of his evil acts. Iago has Roderigo come to Cyprus for this very reason. In the second place, Roderigo is a man who goes to great trouble because of his love for Desdemona, and, in this sense, he shares a motive with the jealous Othello. Finally, Iago's total mastery and manipulation of Roderigo show us how Iago will also be able to master and manipulate the confused Othello. The three victims of Iago's evil — Othello, Cassio and Roderigo — are all powerless to resist the scheming Iago. There is a basic difference, however, in that Roderigo alone knows all along that Iago is scheming; Othello and Cassio are completely unsuspecting. In any case, Roderigo's presence in the play is vital to the development of the plot. At the same time, Shakespeare, through Roderigo, presents us with another of his famous ignorant lovers.

Question 9.

Explain Othello's jealousy and his motivation for killing Desdemona.

Answer

It is easy enough to say that Othello murders Desdemona because he becomes excessively jealous, believing that there is a relationship between her and Cassio. But there is more than sexual jealousy involved. True, the "beast" in Othello is aroused by Iago's suggestions and his erotic tale of Cassio's supposed dream about Desdemona, but is the "beast" really Othello? In a sense, Othello undergoes a transformation back toward the ways of his more primitive ancestry. Othello is a savage who has been tamed through his association with the lords and senators of the republic of Venice. The effect of Iago's schemes is to untame him and release him into a world where acts can be justified by the laws of the jungle. This is demonstrated in the course of the play, particularly in Act III, Scene 3, where Othello, for the first time, almost savagely warns Iago that he had better be telling the truth. It is the beast in Othello that slaps Desdemona in front of Lodovico and the party from Venice. However, in his final moments of rage, Othello is transformed back into a man who is gentle and tender. We see him in his preparation to kill Desdemona as a disturbed man, not an aroused animal. Phrased differently, Othello is reduced to a more animalistic level in the process of becoming more and more jealous, but our final view of him is that of the desperate and unhappy husband.

Jealousy is not the sole explanation for Othello's killing Desdemona. Certainly Othello's honor is involved. We have seen several instances in the play where "reputation" has been given notice and importance. When Othello relieves Cassio of his office as lieutenant, Cassio's immediate reaction is:

Reputation, reputation, reputation! O, I have lost my

reputation! I have lost the immortal part of myself, and what remains is bestial. My reputation, Iago, my reputation!

There is a fear that the loss of reputation leaves man a mere beast — and Othello does not want this to happen to him either.

In Act III, Scene 4, Emilia asks Desdemona about Othello: "Is he not jealous?" Desdemona's reply is, "Who, he? I think the sun where he was born/Drew all such humours from him." Desdemona never thinks Othello is jealous, for she has seen only the attractive, courageous emotions displayed in his behaviour. The simple truth is that she does not know Othello very well and did not know him well when they were married. Emilia asks, "Is not this man jealous?" and Desdemona replies, "I ne'er saw this before./ Sure there's some wonder in this handkerchief:/I am most unhappy in the loss of it." Desdemona has never witnessed any jealousy in Othello, and naïvely believes that the handkerchief is responsible for the change in his behavior. In the same scene, Emilia explains the nature of jealousy to the innocent Desdemona:

But jealous souls will not be answer'd so;
They are not ever jealous for the cause,
But jealous for they are jealous; 'tis a monster
Begot upon itself, born on itself.

Desdemona's immediate comment is simply, "Heaven keep that monster from Othello's mind!" She does not realize her wish is being made too late. While Othello's jealousy has been aroused— and Shakespeare implies it was always there potentially — he nevertheless kills Desdemona out of pride, anger and honor. To make Othello only one more jealous husband is an oversimplification of character and an underestimation of his temperament.

Question 10.
Describe the basic meaning of *Othello*.

Answer
In *Othello*, Shakespeare shows us the ill effects of a base human emotion, jealousy. This general statement can be supported by a brief survey of what happens in the play. Iago, an Italian filled with wickedness — that is, a conventional villain of Elizabethan

drama – convinces Othello that his wife, Desdemona, is being unfaithful by having a secret romance with Othello's lieutenant, Michael Cassio. Brought to a state of jealousy and uncontrollable suspicions, Othello vows to protect his honor by punishing Desdemona. At the end of the play, Othello smothers Desdemona in her bed and then learns that Iago has tricked him into believing that Desdemona had been unfaithful when she had in fact been loyal. Upon discovering Desdemona's innocence, Othello is overwhelmed by guilt and commits suicide. Thus, false jealousy results in the deaths of both Othello and his wife.

In the principal scene of the play, Act III, Scene 3, when Iago is first planting the seeds of jealousy in Othello, he makes a key statement about the nature of jealousy:

O, beware, my lord, of jealousy;
It is the green-eyed monster which doth mock
The meat it feeds on: that cuckold lives in bliss
Who, certain of his fate, loves not his wronger;
But, O, damned minutes tells he o'er
Who dotes, yet doubts, suspects, yet strongly loves!

This is perhaps the central statement of the play. The idea is that jealousy contains a horrible dilemma: one hates and loves at the same time. Othello is very much in love with Desdemona; at the same time, he hates her for being unfaithful. The combination of love and hatred proves too much for any individual, for it thrusts him into a world of contradictions. Notice the agony of uncertainty in Othello's lines:

I think my wife be honest and think she is not;
I think that thou art just and think thou art not.
I'll have some proof. Her name, that was as fresh
As Dian's visage, is now begrimed, and black
As mine own face.

Shakespeare presents in different ways the strange mixture of love and hate that Othello comes to feel toward Desdemona. At no place in the play is the mixture seen more clearly than in the opening scene of Act IV, when Othello tries to bring himself to damn her, while reminding himself of all her good qualities. At the same time as Othello struggles to condemn her, he experiences the extent of his great love for her purity and gentleness. The conversation with Iago, in part, proceeds this way:

> **Othello:** A fine woman! a fair woman! a sweet woman!
> **Iago:** Nay, you must forget that.
> **Othello:** Ay, let her rot, and perish, and be damned tonight; for she shall not live: no, my heart is turned to stone; I strike it, and it hurts my hand. O, the world hath not a sweeter creature: she might lie by an emperor's side and command him tasks.
> **Iago:** Nay, that's not your way.
> **Othello:** Hang her! I do but say what she is: so delicate with her needle: an admirable musician: O! she will sing the savageness out of a bear: of so high and plenteous wit and invention —
> **Iago:** She's the worse for all this.
> **Othello:** O, a thousand thousand times: and then, of so gentle a condition!

The mixture of love and hate is clear, and we both pity and scorn Othello. Little by little, we see the disastrous effects of jealousy growing out of this love-hate formula. Even when Othello is murdering Desdemona, he is filled with love and tenderness. But the point of the play is that jealousy cannot be stopped once it is started and that, once it is started, it can only lead to ruin. Early in the play, Iago announces his scheme to place Othello "into a jealousy so strong/That judgement cannot cure." (Act II, Scene 1, 310–311). The action of the play fulfils Iago's prophecy with swiftness and determination.

Question 11.

How does the theme of jealousy relate to the human power of reasoning? Is this connection logical?

Answer

At the same time as jealousy and its ill effects are being demonstrated, the audience is given a certain amount of information about the uses of human reason. There is a split between witchcraft and wit throughout the play. The powers of reasoning are pitted against the more "magical" powers of love. Just before his suicide, Othello explains that all will have to refer to him as "one that loved not wisely but too well" (Act V, Scene 2, 344). This is the conclusion to a battle of wisdom or "wit" against ignorance that has been continuing throughout the play.

Near the end of the first act, Iago explains to Roderigo that Othello and Desdemona will be undone by his "wit." As he states it, separating Othello and Desdemona becomes a challenge to him and the forces of evil:

> If sanctimony and a frail vow betwixt an erring barbarian
> and a supersubtle Venetian be not too hard for my wits
> and all the tribe of hell, thou shalt enjoy her.

Iago uses his wit, his scheming or cunning, to make it appear that Desdemona is having a secret romance with Cassio. Furthermore, Iago knows that part of his victory will be determined by the extent to which he can successfully lead Othello into "madness." Iago, using human reasoning, wants to undo his opposition by breaking down Othello's power of reasoning. When Iago speaks of driving Othello into a jealousy so profound that even judgment will not work, he hopes to drive Othello "even to madness" (Act II, Scene 1, 320). When Iago instructs Othello to spy on his talk with Cassio, Iago notes that, when Cassio smiles, Othello "shall go mad; and his unbookish jealousy must construe/Poor Cassio's smiles, gestures and light behaviour/Quite in the wrong" (Act IV, Scene 1, 101–104). The "unbookish" jealousy means that jealousy is unlearned, that jealousy is the logical relative of ignorance, just as cunning necessarily requires intelligence. The logical connections cannot be questioned; throughout the play, Iago is pictured as intelligent and Othello as somewhat unintelligent, more physical than intellectual. When Emilia has discovered Othello immediately after he has killed Desdemona, she cries out, "O thou dull Moor" (Act V, Scene 2, 225) and adds, "What should such a fool/Do with so good a woman?" Iago has made Othello act the part of a fool — a jealous fool.

Othello is particularly suited to lose his abilities to reason because he has always put a certain amount of faith in magic. We recall his explanation of the handkerchief to Desdemona:

'Tis true: there's magic in the web of it:
A sibyl, that had number'd in the world
The sun to course two hundred compasses,
In her prophetic fury sew'd the work.

Iago, on the other hand, frequently announces his confidence that wit can overpower magic or, as he states in Act II, Scene 3: ''Thou knows't we work by wit, and not by witchcraft;/And wit depends on dilatory time.'' Thus, the logic of convincing Othello to commit a wrong is easily understood in the thematic connection between jealousy and ignorance. Who is more fit to become jealous than the relatively unintellectual, literal Othello?

Question 12.

Is the theme of deception in the play relatively conventional?

Answer

Shakespeare's development of Iago's deception of Othello has an unusual twist to it in that Othello is a man easily convinced of literal or visible concepts. Because Othello has an unusually heroic past and has always distinguished himself honorably, he feels that all men are somehow honorable. In his extreme personal honesty, he believes firmly in Iago's honesty. Othello, unlike many men, believes that what he sees is true. Near the end of the first act, Iago says of Othello:

The Moor is of a free and open nature,
That thinks men honest that but seem to be so,

The phrase ''that but seem to be so'' is the clue to the unique ability of Othello to be fooled. When Othello and Iago are discussing Michael Cassio, Iago uses this phrase once again:

Iago: For Michael Cassio, I dare be sworn I think that
he is honest.
Othello: I think so too.
Iago: Men should be what they seem; or those that be
not, would they might seem none!
Othello: Certain, men should be what they seem.

Othello, in other words, is a man who puts unusually great

faith in what "seems" to be true. His demand for proof of Desdemona's unfaithfulness is something visible, the "ocular proof" as it is called. This is Othello's final standard for establishing the truth, and, in this sense, he is unusual. The entire theme of deception is, therefore, somewhat unconventional. In most cases, the deception would not be accomplished so easily. The combination of Othello's extreme literal-mindedness and the demands of the play's other equations between jealousy and ignorance makes the presentation of the deception unusually simple.

Question 13.

Is the problem of "reputation" logically connected to the behavior of Othello?

Answer

One of the dramatic conventions of the Elizabethan theater, and of plays involving military people in particular, is the use of an established and familiar code of honor. Such a code of honor practically dictates that a character act in a certain way. Because *Othello* is a military play—in the sense that it is located in Cyprus in preparation for a battle—it is not surprising to find in it a code of honor. All great soldiers—and that includes Othello, simply by definitions established in Act I—wish to act honorably and, in so doing, to protect their "reputation." Shakespeare deliberately introduces the secondary theme of reputation as a part or symbol of the conventional code of honor. Thus, when Iago first suggests to Othello that Cassio may be involved with Desdemona, he introduces the idea of the possible loss of reputation that could come to Othello. Iago says:

Good name in man and woman, dear my lord,
Is the immediate jewel of their souls:
Who steals my purse steals trash; 'tis something, nothing;
'Twas mine, 'tis his, and has been slave to thousands;
But he that filches from me my good name
Robs me of that which not enriches him
And makes me poor indeed.

Othello's fear of the loss of his honor is foreshadowed by

Cassio's reaction to his loss of the rank of lieutenant. Cassio, also a soldier and a man of honor, cries out that he is in agony over the loss of his reputation, making it clear to the audience that this convention is important in the play:

> Reputation, reputation, reputation! O, I have lost my reputation! I have lost the immortal part of myself, and what remains is bestial. My reputation, Iago, my reputation!

That Shakespeare wants to make the point clear is evident in his repetition of the word ''reputation'' six times. Furthermore, this statement fixes the values in the world of *Othello*. ''Reputation'' suggests ''immortality,'' while all other considerations have a ''bestial'' association. The true irony is that Othello must act like a beast to protect his immortality.

Question 14.

To what extent is *Othello* concerned with innocence?

Answer

Desdemona is somehow almost unbelievable to us, and this may be due to her innocence. Our understanding of Desdemona is inhibited by the seeming split between her sexuality and her naïve ways. When she first pleads to the Duke that she be allowed to accompany Othello to Cyprus, her argument is phrased in terms of her desire to be in the physical presence of Othello:

> That I did love the Moor to live with him,
> My downright violence and storm of fortunes
> May trumpet to the world . . .
> So that, dear lords, if I be left behind,
> A moth of peace, and he go to the war,
> The rites for which I love him are bereft me,
> And I a heavy interim shall support
> By his dear absence. Let me go with him.

Desdemona's desire to live with Othello and enjoy her marital relationship is very understandable, particularly since she is a new bride. She is not sexually innocent, however, and this tends to confuse our general understanding of her as *the* innocent figure in the play. Of course, Cassio is innocent, but our affections are reserved for the helpless Desdemona. It is precisely because she is so helpless, as several critics have argued, that we are moved by her, even though we never feel that we know her that well.

When Desdemona is accused of being "false as hell" by Othello in Act IV, Scene 2, she is totally unable to understand what he means. She innocently suggests that he should not be mad at her if there is some distressing news from Venice. After he has called her a whore, she asks herself, "How have I been behaved, that he might stick/The small'st opinion on my least misuse?" When we see Desdemona asking Iago's advice on how to win back Othello, we seem to view her as the very personification of innocence. The mere fact that she approaches "good Iago" is sadly ironic:

> O good Iago,
> What shall I do to win my lord again?
> Good friend, go to him; for, by this light of heaven,
> I know not how I lost him. Here I kneel:
> If e'er my will did trespass 'gainst his love,
> Either in discourse of thought or actual deed,
> Or that mine eyes, mine ears, or any sense,
> Delighted them in any other form;
> Or that I do not yet, and ever did,
> And ever will — though he do shake me off
> To beggarly divorcement — love him dearly,
> Comfort forswear me! Unkindness may do much;
> And his unkindness may defeat my life,
> But never taint my love.

Desdemona is completely unaware of the nature of Othello's anger. She prophetically notes her forthcoming murder, even though she does not understand the reason for it. This seems to be the essence of her innocence: her willingness to die if Othello so decides, even without knowing why. Thus, she tells Emilia to put the wedding sheets on the bed and even instructs her, "If I do die before thee, prithee shroud me/In one of those same sheets." (Act IV, Scene 3, 24–25). Then, finally, she is shown at the peak of innocence as she begins to sing the melancholy death song about the willow.

Her various suggestions that she would love Othello even up to and after her death are proved by her behavior in the last act. When Emilia discovers Desdemona after she has been smothered by Othello, she asks, "O, who hath done this deed?" Desdemona sighs, "Nobody; I myself. Farewell." This is true innocence. This pitiful destruction of innocence is part of the major action of the play. Just as Emilia's coarse and "experienced" ways help us to appreciate, by contrast, Desdemona's innocent ways, so Desdemona's purity of heart and soul make Othello's poisoned spirit that much more detestable. The play is primarily concerned with demonstrating the evil effects of jealousy. This is accomplished in more striking or dramatic terms by having the jealousy unfounded and by having the object of jealousy so extremely loyal and innocent. Desdemona's pure love is so overpoweringly dramatized — to the final extent of her refusing to name Othello as her murderer — that we feel ourselves revolted by jealousy and its ill effects. The play, then, is about innocence only indirectly — only in its vivid contrast to distrust, suspicion and jealousy, "the green-eyed monster."

It could be argued that Othello is actually as innocent as Desdemona. Throughout the play, he has shown himself to be honest, trusting and virtuous. In fact, it is because he is so trusting and naïve that he is so easily manipulated by Iago. But because of his tragic flaw, jealousy, we tend to overlook his basic innocence.

Question 15.

In what ways, besides his code of honor, is Othello defined by conventions?

Answer

To a certain extent, the meaning of the play is contained in the depiction of the central character. Othello "works" according to a code of honor and "reputation." This is part of his characterization as a professional soldier — a type or convention in many plays. When this is established — as it is in the picture of him as a brave soldier and servant of the state in the first act — a second, more important convention takes command: Othello becomes the classical tragic hero, a good and noble man — as defined by Aristotle — who, through some flaw, is led to disaster and death. Othello's flaw is his strong and naïve belief that things are what they seem. Because of this flaw, he is easily convinced of Desdemona's guilt and is moved to disaster. So, the hero fills the requirements of two conventions — the professional soldier and the tragic hero. These conventions allow us to arrive quickly at an understanding of

80

Othello's temperament and behavior. It is through the attention to these conventions and their familiar meaning that Shakespeare is able to make us understand Othello very swiftly.

Question 16.

Is there appropriate emphasis on the theme of *Othello* or is Shakespeare's attention to jealousy excessive?

Answer

One of the stylistic devices in *Othello* is the way in which Shakespeare's presentation of jealousy is made almost equivalent to that emotion. In other words, jealousy is described throughout the play as a monstrous emotion that becomes increasingly more destructive and intense. As jealousy is always growing, so does Shakespeare's presentation of jealousy grow throughout the play. Shakespeare's attention to jealousy is slight in the opening act. Then, in Act II, jealousy moves swiftly to center stage and stays there for the rest of the play. Shakespeare shows us the actual way in which jealousy becomes excessive by giving excessive treatment to jealousy in a variety of speeches — between Othello and Iago, Desdemona and Emilia, Othello and Desdemona, and Emilia and Othello. In short, almost every pairing of the characters in the final acts of the play directs our attention to jealousy, so that the audience becomes as obsessed with the whole idea of jealousy as Othello does. Thus, his intense reactions and his entire behavior seem more logical and even reasonable. When Iago cautions Othello, "O, beware, my lord, of jealousy;/It is the green-eyed monster which doth mock/The meat it feeds on," he is introducing an idea of jealousy that must be enlarged upon throughout the play.

In the next scene, Emilia returns to the idea of jealousy as a monster, cautioning Desdemona, " 'Tis a monster/Begot upon itself, born on itself." Emilia reminds us of the nature of jealousy. The entire play is based on the developing beast of jealousy, and we cannot say that Shakespeare's treatment of it is any more excessive than the emotion itself. The demands of the presentation of jealousy are met through an appropriate emphasis on jealousy in different parts of the play — slight in the beginning, frequent and intense in the end.

Question 17.

Explain the basic imagery of "magic" and "witchcraft" in

Othello. How does this imagery relate to Othello's manner of speaking?

Answer

There is a sharp division between wit and witchcraft throughout *Othello*. We see an association of magic and bizarre supernaturalism in Othello and in his love for Desdemona, while at the same time we see the opposition to this magic presented in the form of wit, particularly in the form of Iago's scheming.

In accordance with the demands of this central split, it is not surprising that we find various references to magic in the images of the play. The magic of the play is linked to Othello's marriage to Desdemona. When Brabantio first learns that his daughter, Desdemona, has eloped with the Moor, he immediately accuses Othello of enchanting her (Act I, Scene 2, 63). When Othello is through with his explanation of how they honorably fell in love, he says, "This only is the witchcraft I have used." (Act I, Scene 3, 169). In these early associations of Othello with witchcraft there is an implication that black people are somehow allied with supernatural or even unnatural abilities. Othello becomes a kind of would-be black sorcerer. He, after all, is from a different background and poses a threat to the understanding of the others. When Othello explains to Desdemona that there is magic in the web of the handkerchief (Act III, Scene 4, 69), he is telling the audience that there is a certain magic both in his relationship to Desdemona and in the entire play. The entire legend of the handkerchief—that she who loses it will lose her husband—is fulfilled by the action of the play. When Desdemona herself says, "Sure, there's some wonder in this handkerchief" (Act III, Scene 4, 101), we realize that she too believes in the magic.

Because of the way in which Othello is associated with magic through the imagery and primarily through the handkerchief, he speaks in a less "witty" way than Iago does. Othello himself draws attention to his plain speech in the first act: "Rude am I in my speech,/And little bless'd with the soft phrase of peace." We are often reminded that Othello can only speak in a fundamental way, and there is, therefore, an association between his charm and his verbal weakness. Believing in magic as he does, it is unnecessary for him to have developed excellent speech. When he realizes at the end of the play that he has been tricked, he feels certain that Iago is a real devil and thus is incapable of being killed.

This belief reveals his superstition. Finally, when he asks to be punished, he speaks in terms of demonic destruction: he asks devils to whip him away and, further, that he be roasted in sulphur. He asks, in other words, for an almost magical death. He has been the victim of a peculiar magic, he feels, from the very beginning; how else can he explain to himself his mistake in killing his wife?

Question 18.

What are some of the other patterns of imagery in *Othello*?

Answer

The central pattern of imagery, one closely connected to the ideas of magic and witchcraft, is that of imprisonment, of evil entrapping good; of Iago, the spider, catching Othello, the fly. In Brabantio's early accusations, he refers to a possible set of ''chains of magic'' that Othello must have used to trap Desdemona. The irony is that Iago is the one trying to wrap Othello in the chains of jealousy. When Cassio is seen taking Desdemona's hand, Iago turns to the audience in an aside and says, ''With as little a web as this will I ensnare as great a fly as Cassio'' (Act II, Scene 1, 169–170). This image of ensnarement is maintained throughout the play. Later, Iago explains how he will use Desdemona's pleas to Othello to be kind to Cassio as a net in which to trap Othello:

> So will I turn her virtue into pitch,
> And out of her own goodness make the net
> That shall enmesh them all.

Iago's busy plans to trap Othello in a net lead the audience to an appreciation of Shakespeare's irony every time Othello says that he is ''bound'' to Iago, as, for example, in Act III, Scene 3, where Othello says to Iago, ''I am bound to thee for ever.'' (line 213). The irony increases when Iago says that he is the one ''bound'' to Othello, as in ''I am your own for ever.'' (line 480). There is a web in which Othello is being trapped, and the irony is broadened when he talks about the magic in the ''web'' of the handkerchief.

Iago is proud of his attempts to snare Othello and is frequently seen laughing evilly on the sidelines whenever he thinks his traps are working, as in Act IV, Scene 1, when he says:

> Work on,

My medicine work! Thus credulous fools are caught;
And many worthy and chaste dames even thus,
All guiltless, meet reproach.

In the last act, after Othello has killed Desdemona and then learned of her innocence, he turns and quietly asks that someone explain to him why he has been "ensnared" in such an evil way: "Demand that demi-devil/Why he hath thus ensnared my soul and body." This is the final statement within the play of the pattern of ensnarement that has been operative throughout. Shakespeare has relied on a fairly conventional image of the spider and the fly to represent the way in which evil ruins good, but Shakespeare's development of the comparison is expert and subtle enough to remain creative in spite of this conventional picture.

A final pattern of imagery is that of chiaroscuro— a term that refers to contrasts of black and white. There is an easily identified symbolism in Othello's blackness, which will be destructive, and Desdemona's whiteness, which represents her innocence and purity. When Desdemona is first described by Cassio to the officers awaiting her arrival at Cyprus, she is considered to be beyond description, "one that excels the quirks of blazoning pens." Further, she is "divine" and "the grace of heaven." (Act II, Scene 1, 60). Throughout the play, we are conscious of Desdemona's pale white skin and the way in which that paleness suggests divinity and innocence. At the same time, Othello talks about his black face and others refer to his blackness. The contrasting images make Othello seem like a gathering dark storm that will burst upon the whiteness or goodness of Desdemona.

Question 19.

Discuss Shakespeare's diction and use of figurative language in *Othello*.

Answer

Shakespeare's diction in the play is designed to develop characterization through manner of speech. Each character's choice of words tells us something about him. Othello admits in simple terms that he is not an elegant speaker and that his vocabulary, for the most part, is that of the soldier. When Othello has decided to punish Desdemona for her supposed unfaithfulness with Cassio, Othello shouts to Iago: "I will chop her into messes" (Act

IV, Scene 1, 211). The words are those of the man described early in the play by Iago as a ''barbarian.''

Cassio's language presents him as a faithful officer and, at times, a lover of the whore, Bianca. Emilia speaks as the experienced wife and woman. She speaks coarsely when explaining her pessimistic view of men and their feelings about women. For example, she explains to the innocent Desdemona:

'Tis not a year or two shows us a man:
They are all but stomachs, and we all but food;
They eat us hungerly, and when they are full,
They belch us.

Each character is given a manner of expression and a particular vocabulary that will help the audience to see clearly the essence of that character. Iago is the most consistently portrayed through such long, villainous, sensuous speeches as, for example, at the end of Act II:

How am I then a villain
To counsel Cassio to this parallel course,
Directly to his good? Divinity of hell!
When devils will the blackest sins put on,
They do suggest at first with heavenly shows,
As I do now: for whiles this honest fool
Plies Desdemona to repair his fortunes,
And she for him pleads strongly to the Moor,
I'll pour this pestilence into his ear,
That she repeals him for her body's lust;
And by how much she strives to do him good,
She shall undo her credit with the Moor.

Iago's speech is typical, particularly the line, ''I'll pour this pestilence into his ear.'' Here, we find Shakespeare using a figure of speech, a hyperbole (an exaggeration). Literally, Iago will pour nothing into Othello's ear; what he will do is offer Othello some spiteful gossip.

A final stylistic consideration to be noted is illustrated by Iago's long speech from which the above quotation is taken. Like so many of the speeches in the play, it is written in blank verse, unrhyming iambic pentameter. The expert use of blank verse is one of Shakespeare's outstanding contributions to dramatic language, for the rhythm becomes hypnotic as the stressed syllables alternate.

Question 20.
Discuss the importance of setting in *Othello*.

Answer
Setting is not as important in *Othello* as it is in *King Lear* and *Macbeth*. The physical surroundings in *Othello* are not often described. There is no enlargement of the scene from the local and realistic to the supernatural. Atmosphere is important, but it arises out of imagery rather than setting.

Nevertheless, the two places in which *Othello* is set are distinguishable. The play opens in Venice; then, at the beginning of Act II, moves to Cyprus for the rest of the action.

Venice is the ultimate base of the action. All of the major characters except Othello and Cassio are Venetians and bring with them to Cyprus what they had become in Venice. Venice represents two things above all: a peaceful, law-abiding city and, according to some evidence, a city of sophisticated customs. The scene with the Duke and senators (Act I, Scene 3) demonstrates the first of these. Venice, despite Brabantio's hysteria over his daughter's elopement, is characterized by wise, impartial judgment, and all of its citizens except Iago are fair-minded, including the exotic and not always intelligible Othello. Concerning the sophistication of the Venetians, we hear about this only from Iago and perhaps from Brabantio's reference to the kind of suitors Desdemona had turned down: "The wealthy curled darlings of our nation" (Act I, Scene 2, 68). Iago calls Desdemona "a supersubtle Venetian" (Act 1, Scene 3, 364). He also tells Othello:

> In Venice they do let heaven see the pranks
> They dare not show their husbands . . .

Nothing in the play proves this, but many in Shakespeare's England had learned from books and returning travellers to distrust Italians for their elegance and cunning. Certainly, we are meant to approve of Desdemona's rejection of courtly and suave Venetian suitors in favor of the Moor, but we are not meant to condemn Venice as significantly overcivilized.

From the peaceful, protected and refined society of Venice, the scene turns to Cyprus, "a town of war,/Yet wild, the people's hearts brimful of fear" (Act II, Scene 3, 213–214). In courageously following her new husband to Cyprus, Desdemona separates herself from her family and culture. When the crisis with her maddened husband occurs, she has no relatives to turn to. Cyprus, for her, brings threatening isolation. Like other islands in Shakespeare, it is also the scene of strange happenings. But these happenings are not supernatural or related to the atmosphere of the place. Without Iago, Cyprus would be a pleasant island.

NOTES